# THE
# WARNING

A novel by
## GEORGE HIRTHLER

*InterVarsity Press*
*Downers Grove*
*Illinois 60515*

InterVarsity Press is the book-publishing division of Inter-Varsity Christian Fellowship, a student movement active on campus at hundreds of universities, colleges and schools of nursing. For information about local and regional activities, write IVCF, 233 Langdon St., Madison, WI 53703.

Distributed in Canada through InterVarsity Press, 1875 Leslie St., Unit 10, Don Mills, Ontario M3B 2M5, Canada.

Cover illustration: Cliff Hayes

ISBN 0-87784-841-6

Printed in the United States of America

**Library of Congress Cataloging in Publication Data**

Hirthler, George, 1947-
　The warning.

　I. Title.
PS3558.I74W3　　　　　813'.54　　　　　81-17225
ISBN 0-87784-841-6　　　　　　　　AACR2

| 17 | 16 | 15 | 14 | 13 | 12 | 11 | 10 | 9 | 8 | 7 | 6 | 5 | 4 | 3 | 2 | 1 |
| 94 | 93 | 92 | 91 | 90 | 89 | 88 | 87 | 86 | 85 | 84 | 83 | 82 | | | | |

*To my mother and father,*
*who taught me the meaning*
*of enduring love*

He came unto his own,
and his own received him not.

*John 1:11*

# CHAPTER

# 1

YOU GET THE IMPRESSION, looking across the gorge, that those parched, open plains and scrawny woodlands are the impoverished descendants of a once lush and florid garden. Somehow the cruel, inhospitable terrain across the river seems an impostor, a scene that doesn't belong. The roll of the land and the interplay of the sky on the horizon make you want to resketch and color in the arid scenery. Something about the shape of the earth in this area—the way the hills rise so quickly and the hardwoods group together—tells you to expect more than your eyes take in. It's as if your perception is lying. The sky calls for beauty, and may have had it once, but the earth now hands it lean, leafless trees and cracked patches of mud. Your intuitions war with your senses, but only for a moment. Finally, the harsh reality of nature overwhelms you, and you realize you're looking at the truth.

And then he appears. He comes wandering aimlessly from among the distraught oaks and pines at the foot of the highest visible mount. It's no more than a half day's journey from the ridge of that mount to the gorge, and as he makes his way down the slope he seems in no hurry. In fact, he seems distracted by things all around him. After ten shuffling steps he turns suddenly to the right and stares for a moment in that direction, searching with his eyes for what? A voice that called his name? A shadow that suggested another presence?

Slowly he turns and begins to move toward the gorge again, his head and body shaking occasionally, turning quickly, signs of the intensity of his thoughts. His pantomime tells you that he is possessed, like so many of us, with a need to know the answers. His struggle is pressing; his need immediate.

Without warning he stops and thrusts his hands high above his head and looks into the vast blue of the sky. At first there is anger in his expression and his fists are tightly clenched. But as he absorbs the serenity of the clouds drifting peacefully above and sees that they are unaffected by his turmoil, the lines of his anger slowly recede, the hardness fades from his face, and his fingers unfold like the petals of a rose and blossom into a plea for mercy. He knows the futility of fighting against those things which he cannot control.

His plea has drawn no obvious answer, and his hands fall to his sides as his gaze returns to the ground. He moves on toward the gorge and the thundering torrents of the Crescent River. For most of his life this river has been a source of strength and peace to Josh Calvert. It's to this river, to the awesome sound of its currents, to the moist touch of its spray, that Josh returns when his struggles are worst. Somehow this river, with its surging energy and its rapid white refusal to slacken its rush, imparts to Josh the feeling that life can be different, will be different if he can just hold fast to the path he's called to follow.

Josh has always known, from the first time he wandered off the farm at the age of seven and found the Crescent waiting, that even this river, as wild and as uncontrollable as it seemed, had not chosen its own course. In its primeval beginnings it was forced to follow the laws of nature into the lowlands and those small valleys that were meant to guide its waters before they ever flowed.

Yes, it had cut deeply into the earth that embraced its torrents, etching its character into even the hardest rock. And yes, those small rivulets had become severe canyons that dropped into a subterranean pathway of blue, but even this river could not escape the path the earth had designed for its magnificent flow.

And thirty years before, when Josh Calvert was born without a voice, his parents knew, because their baby did not cry, that the circumstances that would mark his life were dictated by a fate they couldn't comprehend. They accepted his silence and returned love in good measure, believing that their only child would one day discover a language of his own, and learn to speak with a voice that did not need sound, that required no ear.

In any year other than 1872 the birth of a mute would have drawn great attention and sympathy from the small but busy population of Shiloh. But in 1872 the townspeople were occupied with more pressing concerns. Two months before Josh entered the world, the old wooden train trestle that bridged the Crescent just two miles east of the hamlet had collapsed. All three of the passenger cars on the Mid-West Express plunged into the Crescent's hundred-foot gorge. And as they ricocheted off of the rocks like toys pitched over a cliff, they delivered death to the hundred and twenty people who were on board. After the men of Shiloh retrieved the bodies with the help of a contingent of soldiers sent by the Governor, the state coroner discovered that most of the inhabitants of one of the cars had survived the fall, only to have their lives claimed by the inrushing turbulence of the river.

The tragedy was the worst that ever hit that small western town, far worse than the murder of the sheriff two years earlier. Shiloh might have regained its momentum if it weren't for the railroad's decision.

A couple of months after the catastrophe, at about the time of Josh's birth, the first succeeding train to come down the tracks pulled into Shiloh's station. It was a short two-car Pullman that had a luxurious interior, quite unlike the austere, hard-seated cars that once passed through every week.

There was something ominous about its arrival and the half-dozen black-suited emissaries who debarked when it hissed to a halt. Many of the townspeople congregated on the platform to greet these railroad dignitaries, but their warm-hearted welcome drew only reserved comments and cold stares. Obviously the mission that these tight-lipped gentlemen pursued did not bear the imprint of friendship.

They spent most of their time in quiet discussion in the bar-room restaurant of The Queen, Shiloh's lone hotel. They retired early, stayed only three days and made only two trips to the site of the broken trestle and mangled trains. They seldom spoke and refused to answer those inquisitive enough to ask when the work crews would arrive to repair the overpass.

Finally, the night they left, three of Shiloh's most vocal citizens, Carl Elder, who owned The Queen, Henry Waite, who owned the general store, and Young Thomas, a strapping youth of imposing physical stature, confronted the railroad's officials in the hotel lobby.

It began awkwardly as Carl Elder announced that he was a spokesman for the townsfolk, which he was only by self-appointment, and the six men tried to excuse themselves on the pretense of catching the train. When the men in black hoisted their luggage to move toward the door, Elder nodded to Young Thomas, who stepped forward to block their passage, indicating as he did that their "bloody train could wait." The men understood the tone of Thomas' declaration and set their baggage down.

Drawing strength from this minor victory, Elder demanded to know exactly when reconstruction would begin. The men avoided the issue with sentences about recommendations to those in power and phrases like budgetary restrictions and further fiscal analysis, but their diversions proved unsuccessful when Elder lost his temper and Thomas threw one of them over the registration counter. Several yelled things like you can't do that and you won't get away with this, but when Thomas reached out for another one, their resistance broke. The most frightened among them, a skinny little mustached man, uttered the bad news. The railroad had no intention of dispatching a work crew to Shiloh, he said. The trestle would not be repaired. It was very likely that the Mid-West Express would be rerouted and the train station at Shiloh shut down.

After a few seconds of stunned disbelief, it was Elder and Waite who cried you can't do that and you'll never get away with this. Elder threatened to call his friends in high places and use the Governor to pressure the railroad to change its insensitive corporate mind. Young Thomas articulated his frustration non-verbally. This time he threw two of the railroaders through the hotel doors onto Main Street, a wide dirt road that fronted a dozen wooden buildings and stopped at the train station.

As the six men scurried toward the safety of their plushly decorated Pullman, the shocking news quickly made its way through the community. Within twenty minutes the train had stoked up and begun its long backward journey across the great prairie, and an angry mob had congregated in the lobby of The Queen. Outraged and confused, the people tried to formulate a plan of demands and appeals.

If they failed to persuade the railroad to restore the route to Shiloh, they all knew it was only a matter of time before their town perished. Many trembled and looked with fear to the future, knowing that their lifeline had just been severed.

It was in the midst of this turmoil, when everyone in Shiloh was screaming about injustice, that the baby without a voice was born. Needless to say, nobody noticed. Nobody visited the Calvert farm. Nobody brought gifts, not even the traditional baby afghan that any neighboring mother could have knitted. In a way, Josh's parents were relieved. The obscurity excused the need for the explanations they'd have had to offer.

And so Josh's infancy passed quietly. The first connection between his birth and the railroad accident was voiced by Dolly Elder, Carl's wife. Dolly had come to town a few years before and taken a room at The Queen. Her background was suspect and her habit of hanging around the bar cast further doubt on her character. She formed easy liaisons with several of the townsmen, and it surprised everybody when Carl Elder announced their engagement. At twenty-four she was six years younger than Carl, but had no difficulty sharing his authority.

It was in the bar before a group of men that Dolly made a casual remark about how strange it was that a mute was born when the trains had stopped.

Somebody said something about the kid being a curse and another seconded the motion with the simple statement that that was a possibility. Nobody seemed concerned with the logic of such notions, and before the conversation went much further the fact was established in everybody's mind that young Josh was somehow responsible for what had happened at the time of his birth.

The railroad had proven totally unresponsive to the onslaught of letters, threats and appeals that poured from Shiloh. A handful of families moved away in 1873 and business at the general store and the hotel fell sharply. Only the bar, with its steady flow of complaining men, showed any sign of profit. Long, repetitive discussions only demonstrated that no one in Shiloh had a solution to the problem. Everybody had an opinion, of course, but most were based on emotion and lacked the compelling strength of reason.

One week the idea that the railroad should be robbed would gain popularity, but before too long it would lose ground to another argument. For almost a month Carl Elder had everyone convinced that a gambling casino and house of prostitution would bring the railroad back, but he couldn't find enough support to bring his vision to pass. And as each idea rose and fell, the bitterness and despair mounted. The suggestions became increasingly senseless and the hopelessness almost unbearable, until out of quiet desperation all those in the bar sought refuge in Dolly's unfounded bigotry. The child without a voice, the boy who couldn't talk back, took the blame for all that was wrong in Shiloh. The animosity spread quietly in late-night discussions over dim oil lamps in small back rooms. Slowly and unbeknownst to Josh or his parents, a distrust and hatred grew as his silence strangely mimicked the stillness along the tracks.

Although Josh's parents knew nothing of this malice, they did notice a growing coldness in their contact with people who once responded warmly. Every month their only horse pulled their wagon to town for supplies. In the general store Henry Waite and his wife, Betty, seemed in a hurry to get rid of them. Where there was once convivial greeting and shared laughter, there was now detachment and a terseness that bordered on hostility. It seemed more obvious every visit, and yet the Calverts fought against the temptation to discuss it, knowing that any examination would lead them into criticism of Betty and Henry. But after a year and a half, Josh's mother, Marlene, spoke bluntly to her husband one night after dinner. Their small, isolated cabin cracked with warmth from a fire that Josh's father, Jesse, had just built. Her question cut through their room like a winter breeze.

"Why are Henry and Betty treating us mean?" she asked, a note of desperation in her voice.

Jesse knew she needed reassurance. He wanted to tell

her it was just her imagination, but he could not bring himself to lie. Searching for an explanation, his eyes wandered the windowless room and finally settled on their two-year-old son, who was lying on their big bed playing with a stuffed bear his mother had made for him. Jesse did not say much, but what he said carried the weight of authority and Marlene trusted his simple wisdom. With a strong, quiet manner and unwavering stability, he had won her loyalty.

He broke the gaze he had fixed on Josh and said in a sympathetic way, "Honey, they're just hurtin' 'cause the railroad took away a lot of their business. It's only natural for folks to get a little moody when their fortunes change. We just need to be patient and see them through this thing."

She accepted his pronouncement without reservation, and when he came to her and wrapped her in his warm, manly hug, she let go of the fear that had bothered her that day. Something in the security of their embrace released her burden, and its weight rose from her shoulders and disappeared like the heat that raced up the chimney. In their simple way they told one another that there was really nothing to fear. And later that night as they drifted together into the sweet peace of sleep, she thought she heard him gently whisper not to take it personally.

# CHAPTER

# 2

ALMOST FIVE YEARS LATER, still facing the town's un-quenched hostility with shared optimism, Marlene and Jesse decided to enter Josh into Shiloh's school. Less than a dozen children attended the Abraham Lincoln Elementary School, and all of them were older than Josh. His parents knew there would be difficulties, but they also had confidence in Josh's ability, even though he seemed reluctant to learn to read or write. On the farm he did his chores with smiling vigor. He proved an able assistant, strong for his six years, when he helped his father uproot the trunk of an old oak tree. Jesse often said that Josh didn't need the continual overseeing Marlene gave him. School would be a chance for their voiceless boy to "learn a few things for himself."

Since Josh knew none of the other children except at a distance, Marlene arranged a Saturday afternoon birthday party at the farm. She didn't want him to enter school totally unacquainted. Two weeks before the party, she sat down with Josh and wrote short invitations to each of the other children in Shiloh. On each one Josh left an inky print and listened attentively as she told what she knew of their personalities. She called Lisa Miller "a pretty little blonde thing" and Henry Waite, Jr.," a bit of a ruffian, but a good-hearted boy nonetheless."

Josh's eyes brightened with each description, and his mother was pleased with the happiness she saw on his face. He showed no fear of meeting the other children, which encouraged her greatly as she planned her son's social debut.

Jesse made a special trip to the general store, and hand-delivered all eleven invitations to Henry Waite, asking him to see that they reached their intended recipients. Since the post office had closed, Henry did this sort of thing freely and accepted the small stack of envelopes with a hint of a smile.

That week Jesse butchered a pig, salted it and hung it in the shed to cure for cooking. The day before the party Marlene baked a cake and filled the cabin with the rich aroma of chocolate. Wild roses were cropped and hung decoratively on Friday afternoon. Saturday morning Marlene and Jesse got up at daybreak to start the ham, make the punch and finish cleaning up. They thought Josh was sleeping late up in the loft, but he lay awake savoring the first moments of this special day.

When he finally climbed down, his mother fixed him a bowl of sweet oats and told him what a wonderful day it would be. No sooner was he finished eating than he dashed outside and ran straight across the barnyard to their rickety old windmill.

Marlene tried to stop him, shouting, "Josh, you stay down from there."

But Jesse said, "Let him go. He'll be all right." And together they watched their seven-year-old climb the skinny structure that pumped water from the earth.

Josh loved the windmill, loved to sit on its scant little platform, feeling on his face the breezy backwash from its lazy turning blades. He liked it above the cabin and barn, and although his precarious perch caused his mother fright, Josh never felt fear; the wind always seemed so friendly.

This morning he wanted to be the first to see his guests coming. He wanted to climb down and gesture their arrival to his parents. He fixed his gaze like an eagle on the farthest visible point of the old farm road and determined not to blink until he saw the first wagon. But after an hour he found himself looking over the woods, gazing at the barn, wondering why his mother kept poking her head so nervously out of the cabin door.

The sun moved to the middle of the sky, but nothing moved on the road. Josh climbed down, trying to make sense of the thoughts that raced through his mind. In the cabin, he could hardly face his parents who were having trouble facing each other.

By nightfall none of the guests had shown up and Josh ran off into the woods wishing he could scream "no, no, no," back to his parents, who pleaded with him to return. He looked back once, saw his mother framed in the distant light of the cabin's doorway, turned and plunged deeper into the night.

He ran wildly, without direction, away from the broken

dream of new friendships. His arms and face were cut by branches and thorns that grabbed at him from the black shadows of the woods. He felt the blood running and then drying on his face as he ran from the memory of his mother's refrain, "Don't worry, Josh, they'll be here any minute." He remembered looking at his father, all the time standing by the door, awfully silent, something ugly rising inside of him. His legs and pants felt damp with the blood of many small cuts, but he ran on anyway, further and further from the stinging disappointment of his rejection. His chest burned now with the need to rest. His legs ached from the strain of several miles. But he refused to stop, tears streaming from his eyes, anger and sorrow swelling in his heart. He raced on in the darkness across patches of open prairie and farmlands, through glades of hardwoods and pines, in and out of moonlit shadows, moving swiftly without direction, a young runner driven toward an uncertain finish line.

Suddenly, in the middle of a long stride his foot caught something dark and heavy and his body pitched forward, twisting in the air before crashing down on a bed of snapping twigs and dry pine needles. In the stillness of the woods his thoughts caught up with him. Laying there, breathing in heavy gasps, he thought of that pretty little blonde thing and the good-hearted ruffian.

He wanted to be with them and watch them and listen to the way they took to life. Half-exhausted, but painfully alert, he could imagine what it would have been like if they had come to him. He felt as if he could almost have talked to them, maybe even have explained what life was like without a voice. Oh, how he wished they would have come and stopped the pain he saw in his mother's face as the sun finally set.

He thought again of each of them and found, as he pictured their faces, that same fascination and attraction taking hold on his heart. A smile etched its way around the corners of his mouth as he imagined himself in the midst of them, a friend among friends. He wanted so much to become one of them but he didn't know how and his mind began to fall again into the fear that there was no way to make them understand that ... that what? That he needed them? No, that wasn't it. His pull toward them was rooted in something else, but what? What was it that drew him to want to be so close to them? He wondered.

And he decided that somehow he would show them that his party didn't matter. They could still be friends. Yes, they would be friends. He would find a way to draw them close and bring them together over the bridge of his silence. With the heat of this revelation flooding through his body, he got to his feet to go back to the farm and gesture this news to his parents.

Cautiously stepping forward, Josh was suddenly aware that he had no idea which way he had come. In his flight he had lost all sense of direction. He had never wandered so far on his own before. After a dozen quick steps he felt the ground begin to incline. Remembering how fast he'd been moving just before he fell, he figured he had raced down this hill and began to retrace his imagined path.

It was a short climb to the top, which passed without incident. At the ridge the air cooled slightly and Josh heard an unusual sound. At first he was struck with fear because the sound carried with it, even though it seemed distant, the power of thunder. But the fear quickly turned into curiosity. This was something else.

Josh listened intently to this new sound as it rode the cool breeze that carried up the ridge. He stood still and concentrated for a couple of minutes, his sensitive ears straining to discern the source of the rumble. Steadily, and with little variation, it beat softly on his waiting ears. The fear had subsided completely and Josh knew that this was not a hostile sound. Its power was soothing, even inviting, not menacing like a thunderstorm.

He moved cautiously downhill, toward an unknown attraction. With each step the sound became more coaxing. Josh began to pick up layers of sound, a depth and texture that enchanted his sense of hearing. He moved a little quicker, realizing that the sound was now coming at him from both sides. It had surrounded him with a clamoring repetition. And in the darkness he knew he was close to the source of an awesome force, a presence that had roared forth for centuries, unstoppable and unceasing in its furious rush.

Josh was suddenly compelled to stop and sit down. On the ground his fingers felt a light dew and in the air he smelled a freshness that made him want to breathe faster and deeper. A slight gust of wind brought a wave of moisture to his face. He rested against a fallen tree and let the deafening noise lure him into sleep. He knew that when the sun woke him his eyes would feast for the first time upon the river he had heard his father call a killer.

# CHAPTER

# 3

AT THE AGE OF THIRTY, Josh Calvert still found fascination in the blue-white currents of the Crescent. And now as he approached it through the parched woodlands on the east side of Shiloh, he hoped he would find in its rushing rhythms the peace he sought, the answers he desperately needed.

There were times when his need to communicate grew intense. And this was one of them. Deep in the core of his being, thirty years of unspoken thoughts boiled like the lava of a rumbling volcano. A lifetime of pent-up feelings swelled like the waves of a wind-driven sea, but they found no shore to wash against. In Josh's life there was no release for the unexpressed emotions that waged an unending war for escape.

In those rare moments when he encountered a sympathetic heart—when someone actually sat still long enough to let Josh pantomime a thought—a dam broke somewhere inside and thousands of things he wanted to say gushed into his mind all at once. His desire to show his love was swept away by a flood of confusion that robbed him of his chance to express anything clearly. Outwardly his confusion took the form of wildly conflicting gestures. Before he could control his excitement the sympathy in his listeners had turned to fear. Josh knew why they all walked away so quickly: they thought he was crazy. And he knew no way to convince them he was sane.

The emotional pain hadn't been so bad before his mother died. But in the three years since her death, and in the six since his father had died, the frustrations became worse and worse. While she was alive, Josh had a way of saying things, even though he never learned to read or write. She could look into his eyes and understand what was on his mind. She read his heart in the look on his face. The way he stood and sat and moved told her things about his mood. She even made sense of the rhythm of his breathing. It seemed to Josh that her understanding was unlimited, that she possessed a secret motherly wisdom that let her look directly into his soul. He loved the way she interpreted the motions of his hands, always so precise as she spoke out loud the thoughts he waved silently through the air. Her smile was everpresent when he was telling her about something he had seen in the woods, by the river, or in Shiloh itself, where he would often wander. She could detect the shades of meaning in the movement of his fingers. Without any training their years together had given them a language of their own. And Josh believed what his mother had told him so often—that others could understand him and see that he was good and full of love if only they would learn to listen with their hearts.

But she was gone now and he had come across no one like her.

Again he stopped as he came to the edge of the gorge and thrust his hands up to the sky in search of a sign or answer. He had learned to live with her death just as he had learned to live without a voice, but he never completely understood why she had to die when she did or why he couldn't talk. Usually it did not bother him, but there were times when he couldn't keep those questions out of his mind.

Like that morning—when he rose to pray as he normally did at the start of every day—his eye caught sight of his clothing. Hanging from a pegboard his father had made years before, were his overalls, flannel shirt and wool coat. He spotted a hole in the left elbow of his shirt.

Instead of getting on his knees to pray, he got up to take a closer look at this new problem. Taking the red-and-white plaid flannel in his hands, he noticed other smaller flaws that he hadn't seen before. The collar was threadbare, and the cuffs were frayed and darkened by dirt. His overalls needed mending, and his coat was ripped too. Josh knew how to use a needle and thread, and he decided to do his stitching when he hand-washed everything at the end of the week.

But as he turned back toward his bed, the bed his parents had once used, his eyes were filled with the disarray of his cabin. Dirty plates and food crumbs littered his table. His floor gave plenty of evidence of the mud caked on his boots. Plants that were kept just inside the door had withered and died in their pots. In the shadows, cobwebs and dust reminded him that the cabin never looked this bad when his mother was alive. She took care of all these things.

But his once cheery home, alive with the animation of his mother's ceaseless activity, now sat motionless, gathering the dust that silently settles everywhere.

He dressed hurriedly and went out to face the sun, but the light of day fell on the weeds that sprouted in the pasture, the broken hinge on the barn door, and the small corral fence that badly needed repair. Josh turned and walked away from it all. The poverty and hopelessness of his life filled his thoughts. Soon he could see only the problems, the absences, the void left by the deaths of his parents. He wandered through Shiloh on his way to the Crescent, knowing that his tattered appearance, his stubbly beard and messy black hair would offend those who saw him and confirm their opinion that he was crazy.

At the river again, with hands in the air, pleading to the God that his mother said was merciful, Josh fell to his knees in tears. So badly he wanted to look into a face, to send love to another human being and have it received with a smile and a hint of comprehension. He cried without sound, wondering when, pleading that he might find someone who would listen.

He had come to the Crescent for solace and was now unaware of its thundering presence. He fell prostrate into the dust high above its roaring waters. His thoughts consumed him. As he rose to his feet, he staggered momentarily, wiping his eyes with the back of his fingers. He lost his balance slightly, felt himself leaning forward and stepped out to counterbalance his motion.

Where there should have been ground there wasn't. Josh opened his eyes just in time to realize that he had stepped into a break in the cliff, a V that nature had notched into the upper reaches of the gorge. He stretched out, desperately trying to stop himself, but his grasp clutched only air. He plunged into the opening above the hungry torrents waiting below.

His body somersaulted once as it catapulted toward the Crescent. He watched the cliffs and the sky twirl by wildly as he spun through this final orbit. In the instant before he hit, he caught a glimpse of his onrushing destination. It wasn't water he beheld; it was rock. He tensed his body for the crush of death, picturing the smooth surface of the granite outcropping he had just seen. But as he twisted helplessly again and his eyes had one last look at the fullness of the sky, his body slammed into the white rapids of the Crescent.

For one eternal moment, he felt relief. His limbs telegraphed the best of all possible news: I'm alive. But that instantaneous revelation was wiped out as quickly as it had arrived by a shocking wave of pain. The surface of the water, before it broke and sucked him down, met Josh with an unforgiving sting. He had fallen almost a hundred feet and landed flat on his back. The concussion knocked the wind out of him. And as the waters spread to take him down, wild panic overwhelmed him. His mouth was open but he couldn't breathe.

Suddenly, he was under. Like a large greedy hand, a swelling torrent spread over his body and yanked him down into the silent but mighty undercurrent. He was careening along the rocky riverbed, twirling in a haphazard, ceaseless motion. He clutched at the bottom, but his hands were torn away before he could grip anything. Abruptly his body pitched sideways in the current, and his outstretched arm was bent against his back as he bounced helplessly off an underwater boulder. A sharp burning pain spread in his chest, like a white ember radiating fire. It crept into his throat. Josh knew he could breathe, but now there was no air. With renewed violence the Crescent sucked him deeper into its surging flood.

The river that had been his companion for so many years now held his life and seemed intent on taking it. Josh fought its treachery, knowing that he could only last a few more seconds against this cruel betrayal. The fire in his chest would soon ignite an explosion that would leave his body limp, floating like debris in the eddies downstream, his white-washed bones turned finally into driftwood and sediment. With a last burst of energy, he tried to thrust his legs against the bottom, but he failed and his head richocheted violently off another unseen boulder.

Then there was sound, the familiar rush of the rapids. And he felt himself falling again, back into a sluice in the river that had just spit him into the air as its current dove over a short waterfall. He sucked and his lungs nearly burst with fresh air. But his escape was momentary and again the Crescent pulled him down, wrapping him in its coils like a determined boa constrictor.

The air restored his fight. He struggled to gain a sense of balance, but the undertow battered his body into submission. Then he was up again, riding the swift surface on his back. He tried to roll over, to drag himself toward the bank, but the Crescent drove him instead across its twisting current. For a second he caught sight of the haunting remains of the old train trestle and one mangled passenger car. A voice from the past reminded him that the Crescent was a killer, and he struggled to find a way of escape. But the river sucked him under again. A silent scream burst through his mind as he knifed straight into its depths.

This time his feet hit bottom, but the river quickly robbed him of a chance to spring up. Its force recognized no resistance. Josh bent beneath the weight of its power, now unable to control even the smallest physical movement. In a whirling rush the undertow spun him along the deepest part of the river's channel. Again and again his body ricocheted off crude hard shapes that intruded into the flow he was forced to follow. His sense of balance now completely gone, he felt himself being whipped against the undertow, as if he had been shot like a bullet through the current. And then he was in the air again, falling past the empty tomb of an old railroad car stacked on its end when it plummeted over the precipice of the broken trestle.

He fell past the shattered windows that once reflected the panicked faces of men and women screaming to their deaths. In the empty car he saw the splashing image of the Crescent's lethal fingers. And in an instant, as the water churned through an opening, he saw what appeared to be a face looking back at him, strangely serene, a familiar countenance that he recognized. The face seemed to be his own.

Once more he went under, this time closing his eyes in exhaustion, accepting the watery grave that fate had prepared. His life played its final scenes in memories that danced across his vision while his body pounded unconsciously against the dark and unrelenting weapons of the river.

# CHAPTER

# 4

HE WOKE WITH A SHARP PAIN in his lower back. His eyes wouldn't focus, but he could hear the rapids rushing all around him. The pain came again. He gritted his teeth and jerked his head back, and it thudded against something sturdy. Compressing his facial muscles and eyelids, he strained to make sense out of the patterns of light bombarding his retinas. Slowly his vision cleared and he found himself suspended above the Crescent, hanging horizontally just above its mighty rush, pinned against the stalk of a fallen tree.

His arms were tangled in a jungle of limbs and driftwood, a natural dam formed by the rise and fall of the river. His right leg hung over the stalk that pressed against his back and his left leg hung down into the Crescent, which flowed only a foot beneath his hanging body. The pain came again. Josh wrenched his neck and pulled his left arm down through the water to untangle it. With one arm free, he hoisted himself up onto the thick trunk of the tree. Feeling his back with numb fingers he discovered a rip through his water-soaked coat where the pain seemed to center. It was a puncture but not serious. Josh found the source of his wound when he spotted blood on the tip of a broken branch protruding from the tree.

Aches rose and fell in every part of his body and he shivered slightly, although the noonday sun promised to dry and warm him. The tree was his bridge to safety, for it led to a small patch of sand at the edge of the water. Carefully, he crawled away from the threat of the Crescent's turbulence and let himself collapse on the sandy bank. The sun performed its kind service, and warmth crept back into his body. He slept in exhaustion, his left foot extended into the shallow edge of the water.

Later, when he began to stir, warm winds swept across the shining, bright surface of the river and tickled the sand that stuck to his cheek. He woke fully and set his arms to push himself to his knees, but he hesitated when his eyes caught hold of an unusual piece of driftwood that lay alone in the sand, about six feet further ashore. An ache in his back reminded him of the trial he had just survived, and he pushed against the ground, rising without difficulty to his knees.

Sitting in the sunlight, propped against the fallen tree that saved him, Josh gazed upstream, wondering why the river let him live. His eyes pierced the rapids and rolling white foam, and his gaze covered the punishing rocks that lurked at every turn of the stream. He felt a deeper kinship toward the river. There was a mystery in their relationship, an unspoken bond that had been strengthened, not violated, by their tortuous encounter. Further upstream he could still see the wreckage of the Mid-West Express, a bad memory from which Shiloh had yet to be delivered. He remembered the tragedy and wondered why the river had refused even one survivor then, only to let him live now.

With these thoughts running through his mind, his eyes were pullled again to that short piece of driftwood. There must have been hundreds of broken branches jammed into the natural dam he leaned against, and yet this piece lay apart, resting on the undisturbed carpet of golden sand that sparkled in the bright afternoon sun. It was only about two feet long and stained dark brown by being in the water for who knows how long. There was something about its shape that held Josh's gaze as he tried to remember why it seemed so familiar.

Just then a shadow passed over the sand between Josh and the stick. He looked up in time to see a bird, smaller than a hawk, silhouetted against the bright sky, ascending the heights of the gorge. It flew out of sight over the ridge, and his gaze fell again to the driftwood.

He crawled closer but didn't touch it. He saw in it lines that formed a specific shape, like a natural wood sculpture. Somewhere in the roots of his memory an image began to form. But he couldn't see it clearly. He turned the driftwood over, studied it and considered the impression it was making on him. Slowly the image began to form in his mind, and the wood on the sand and the clarity of his thought were suddenly connected. Then his mind and body were flooded with the light of revelation.

Instantly he experienced a joy he had never known before because he knew his prayers had finally been answered. He lifted the driftwood out of the sand and held it above his head in an offering of thanks. On his knees he clutched it to his chest and wept. For Josh Calvert knew, as clearly as he knew anything, that in this simple piece of driftwood he had finally found his voice.

For an hour he stayed on that sandy patch of ground, controlling an impulse to run into Shiloh and share his discovery with the townspeople. He stayed to pray and thank God for such a marvelous gift. And as he did, his strength returned. Over and over again he called to mind a verse from the Old Testament that his mother was fond of quoting. It was from the book of Isaiah and he knew now that it was always meant for him. "They that wait upon the LORD shall renew their strength; they shall mount up with wings as eagles; they shall run, and not be weary; and they shall walk, and not faint."

And as he prayed and grew in strength, he couldn't keep his mind off the faces of the people in Shiloh. For so many years he had pleaded for one, just one, who would listen. But now he had something so much better than a single listener, now he had a message that was meant for all of them. And he knew they'd understand. He knew he could make them understand, for this was his chosen mission. The reward for thirty years of silence had arrived. It all culminated the moment his eyes fell upon that driftwood. For the first time he understood why he had to endure a life apart, so different and so distinct. Josh now understood that he had been entrusted with a message of hope for the people of Shiloh. An oracle, a miraculous sign was being sent through him. His life had been spent in preparation, and now they would know he wasn't insane. They would see that he held a promise in which everyone could share. It might have taken him a moment to understand the mystery in the driftwood, but they would see it instantly.

Josh was running now, excitedly, hardly aware of the pain that only hours before had rendered him unconscious. Leaping from one rock to another, darting across stretches of open shore, he made his way swiftly along the bottom of the gorge. In his right hand he clutched the source of his excitement, an inconspicuous piece of waterlogged wood that resembled the batons that runners used in relay races. To Josh it was more like a scroll from heaven, a revelation he couldn't wait to unfold for others.

He leapt over a small canal in the riverbank and sprinted along the shoreline next to the mangled railroad cars. Stopping for a moment to find his way out, he raised the stick to the sky again in a gesture of thanks.

That part of the old trestle that did not collapse, that part that was fixed to the wall of the gorge, offered Josh a crude, but plausible, stairway to the ridge. Mounting an old crossbeam, he crawled and climbed his way up through the wooden structure of supports that once bridged the Crescent.

When he finally hauled himself out of the gorge, he walked out on the short section of track that still extended out over the cliff. His eye traced the path that the train had taken. The iron rails curved apart where they bent down into the gorge, hanging in the air like two rusted elephant tusks suspended forever in that last haunting position of tragedy. Josh looked down into the river and followed its course to the fallen tree that had saved his life. From this height it looked almost minute in the midst of the Crescent's motion. He wondered how it had possibly snatched him from the waters of death. When he was on the little beach he couldn't see what was now visible. That tree didn't even cross half the river, and the current easily skirted around its end. A look of fear crossed his face when he realized how easily he might have been carried downstream.

But that was never meant to be, he thought, glancing at the driftwood in his hand. This was meant to be, he reasoned with quiet assurance. With a smile on his face, Josh turned and began to move along the unused tracks that passed through Shiloh. He gave no thought to his appearance as his long strides carried him closer and closer to the town. His clothes were still damp and dirtied by patches of mud. His hair was matted and filthy. And all over, on his hands and cheeks and clothes, were traces of black soot that had rubbed off the trestle supports.

It was less than two miles from the trestle to the town, and when he passed from a thickly wooded stretch and rounded the bend that brought Shiloh into view, a fresh surge of adrenalin pumped through his veins. If he had a voice, he'd have yelled to announce his arrival. Instead, he approached unannounced, but ready nevertheless, to deliver his message to everyone.

# CHAPTER

# 5

IN 1865 WHEN THE UNION PACIFIC Railroad bridged the Crescent and laid track across the great prairie to the mountains further west, nothing but sagebrush and hardwood mounds marked the site of Shiloh.

But the railroad created frontier opportunities and the immigrants from the teeming ghettos of the East's big cities were often the first to take advantage of the open space along the tracks. German and Irish immigrants had settled farms in the plains just west of the Crescent. The river itself was too wild to be tamed for trade. Nevertheless, the farmers increased in number and the land began to yield an abundance of wheat. It wasn't long before the farmers labored together to build a grain elevator that loaded their crops into the railroad's hopper cars. The three-story structure was joined to a small, one-room office where the farmers kept records of who shipped how much wheat.

That little office quickly became the home of a telegraph,

whose thin wires were mounted on poles along the railroad tracks. Soon the immigrants were sending messages to the cities up and down the line, ordering supplies and reporting the fruits of the harvest. Next to the grain elevator they erected a water tank and a gigantic windmill, equipped with a hundred blades to propel it. They intended to harness the power of the prairie wind and to convince the railroad that their little patch of land should become a regular stop. The railroad cordially responded, sending out an ambassador to christen the windmill, which was designed to water the thirsty steam engines that rolled by with some regularity.

At the christening they agreed to call their area Shiloh. Not long after that a man named Mueller and his son spent a full day painting their chosen name in enormous white letters high on the side of the weather-beaten wood-frame grain elevator. When Mueller and his son finished and climbed down from their scaffolding, all of the farming families gathered outside the little telegraph office to celebrate, and the wires carried the news of the birth of their town.

The Irish were Catholics, the Germans Lutheran, but a pioneering spirit pulled them together and they built a beautiful, white frame church with a cross high above a peaked tower that enclosed the front door at its base. The Lutherans held services on Sunday mornings and the Catholics took over in the afternoon. The farmers, bound by their love of the earth, shared their lives congenially.

The church sat about two hundred yards from the tracks, the grain elevator and the windmill. It became the anchor of Main Street, which soon had a row of wood frame buildings on both sides of the dirt thoroughfare, some with porchlike walkways and awnings.

An enterprising young businessman from St. Louis saw that the farmers of Shiloh could easily support a general store. His venture went up across the street from the church. It took the shape of a one-story building with a high, flat-topped facade that read "Waite's General Store" in huge letters and "Tobacco, Soap, Drugs, Hardware and Home Supplies" in smaller letters underneath. Henry Waite and his bride, Betty, made their home in the rooms behind the store. Within a few years the town sported a livery stable run by a blacksmith named Hoffer and a bank set up by a Mr. Williams.

A post office, a row of homes and a restaurant were all built along Main Street in the late 1860s. At the same time a sawmill and lumberyard opened behind the church and construction began on a formal railroad station with a large platform and waiting room. The telegraph was moved into the station house, which sat across Main Street like a blockade at the end of the road.

Horse-drawn buggies entered Main Street from an opening between Waite's store and the church, or they came along the tracks past the grain elevator and cut between the livery stable and the new station.

During those first years there was always lots of activity along the street. To the people who saw Shiloh spring up out of nothing, it appeared the progress would never end. Mr. Williams, the banker, lent the farmers all the money they needed for more horses, and the mood of prosperity saturated the town.

At the high point of Shiloh's modest boom, a man stepped off the train who promised to bring even more growth to the little prairie town. His name was Carl Elder and he talked about the future as if he were standing on the site of the next St. Louis. His boisterous manner overwhelmed the humble immigrants and their quiet families. In short notice most of the news in Shiloh centered around Elder's latest pronouncements and acquisitions. No sooner had he purchased The Griddle, Shiloh's lone restaurant, than he announced plans to expand it into a saloon and erect a hotel on the site. Before it was finished, The Queen, a three-story monument with an arcade roofline and a handrailed balcony skirting the second story, totally dominated Shiloh's skyline. It rose only a few feet shorter than the church steeple, but its width and depth so far outstripped anything else in the city that it looked strangely out of proportion. It was situated halfway between Waite's General Store and the train station, across the street from the post office and a small row of storefront homes where a doctor, barber and leatherworker owned shops.

Elder filled its rooms with itinerant workers, an occasional businessman and those who came to town to try their hand at a game of poker at The Queen. Nobody particularly liked the idea of gambling in Shiloh, but at the town meetings, which were held in a hall built for civic functions by Elder, his interests were always well supported. He agreed not to import prostitutes, but refused to close the door of The Queen to unescorted women. The trade brought in by Elder's business triggered continued growth, but it also brought Shiloh's first crimes. After several robberies and blatant cases of assault, the townspeople insisted on law and order. Funds were raised for a sheriff's office and jail, which were eventually built next to the town hall, between the livery stables and the post office.

The town council, under the leadership of Chairman Elder, hired a sheriff from Kansas. His name was Charles Macklin. Shortly after his arrival rumors circulated that he had worked for Elder before, but not as a lawman. Suspicions were put to rest, however, when Macklin proved to be a gentleman who handled the duties of sheriff with swift precision. Although he developed no personal attachments, Macklin earned the distant respect of Shiloh's residents. When he voiced his opinions at town meetings, they demonstrated both independence and authority. He was one of the few people who openly opposed Elder's positions, and became, as a result, a source of hope to those farmers who weren't at peace with Shiloh's slipping reputation.

The last building erected on Main Street housed a printing press. By then, there were several small streets behind the main thoroughfare, dotted by random homes, craft shops and the town's pride and joy, a one-room schoolhouse. Shiloh's population, including the outlying farming families, surpassed a thousand that year and the city was ready for a newspaper.

A printer from Philadelphia by the name of Hammond moved in and set up shop. Within a year, he and his wife built the circulation of their Shiloh Sentinel to over five hundred copies a week. Hammond reprinted news from Philadelphia and Denver and filled the twelve-page tabloid with stories about local events. Hammond had a distaste for obituaries, "the worst news," but his wife found it easy to compose sensitive stories about all of Shiloh's funerals. She was always on the scene because the small cemetery, with its short picket fence, took up the open space between the Sentinel's office and the church.

The town's growth did, however, quietly level off. The Hammonds noticed because their circulation dropped a little. They never reported it, but since no stable industry had moved to Shiloh, its limited prosperity rose and fell in cycles controlled by the four seasons.

Aside from the long process of reconstruction and the problems of the Union Army's occupation of the South, nothing much grabbed the headlines in those days. In 1868 the Hammonds gave birth to a six-pound fifteen-ounce baby girl. Two years later the murder of the sheriff shocked the town.

But it was another story that started in that year that bore an omen of Shiloh's troubled future. A drought hurt the crop yield badly, and many farmers lost a good part of their income. More often than not, the hopper cars that came for grain, went away half empty. The record books in the little office next to the grain elevator recorded it as the worst harvest in the town's short history. But 1871 proved even worse; the drought continued.

The next year, when the trestle collapsed, the drought still hadn't broken, but most of Shiloh's farmers had. The sky simply refused to release the water of life, and yet the Crescent flowed as always with a fierce surge of irony. When the railroad decided to reroute to the north, bequeathing to Shiloh a death by attrition, the people began to look elsewhere for their livelihood. The population had already dwindled to a mere six hundred, but the stalwarts and perennial optimists stayed. Together they watched the city atrophy, until the last dim ray of hope flickered out.

Thirty years later, those who remained weren't quite prepared, were in no state of mind to receive the enthusiastic lunacy that Josh Calvert was about to spring on them.

# CHAPTER

# 6

THE SKY WAS CLEAR AND BRIGHT as Josh covered that last quarter-mile. Beyond the town he could see the vast, open prairie and the mountains that rose to the west. His eyes traced the fading line of tracks and the ever smaller poles that carried the telegraph wire out over the level landscape.

Just as the street came fully into view between the church and general store, the movement of a windmill caught his eye. The wind fanned its blades slowly against the pure blue sky and Josh broke his pace to match its lazy turn.

A few people, not many, were moving in the street when Josh arrived. A farmer and his wife were loading supplies into their buggy just outside Waite's store. A group of schoolchildren were dispersing down by the livery stable, going their separate ways home. In front of The Queen, two men sat in chairs on the boardwalk, occasionally talking, but saying little. Another empty buggy sat in front of the Sentinel.

Josh came to a disappointed halt just by the corner of the church. He had hoped there would be more people, but he looked again at his stick, held it up in front of his face and knew that even one would be enough. With open eyes and a wide smile, he jogged toward the farming couple. The woman, in her long, full dress, bonnet and shawl had already mounted the wagon. Her husband, having helped her up, was rounding the horse when he noticed Josh coming toward them.

The man turned his back to Josh and climbed up onto the buggy seat next to his wife. Taking the reins in hand, he was about to snap his horse forward when Josh's frantic wave turned his head. Josh kept coming and didn't stop until he stood next to the horse, in front of the wagon wheel at their feet.

"What do you want, Josh?" the farmer asked.

"Let's go home," his wife said before Josh could gesture an answer. He turned his face up to the woman, and she looked down into his eyes. She saw the plea on his face, saw the love in his smile and for a moment sat transfixed with her husband as Josh lifted his piece of driftwood up toward them. Josh shook his head up and down in a wild affirmation and his hands began to tremble, the short shaft of wood vibrating between them.

"That's very nice, Josh," the man said, a note of impatience creeping into his voice.

Josh pivoted slightly, more toward the woman, and thrust the wood up with both arms in her direction; then swung it quickly back toward the man, who couldn't understand what Josh wanted.

"That's nice, Josh. Do you want us to have it? Is it for

us?" he asked, stretching forward to take hold of it. But Josh pulled back, shaking his head no.

"Let's go home; he's filthy," the woman said. But Josh stood in the way of the wheel, again lifting the driftwood toward them, now breathing and exhaling in gasps as if he were desperately trying to talk.

"Look out, Josh!" the farmer yelled, cracking the reins across the horse's back, fleeing the awkward confrontation with the mute.

Josh jumped back as the wheel rolled at him. The wagon kicked dust up out of the ruts in the dry street and the door of the general store swung open. Henry Waite emerged and stood on the wooden walkway about six feet from Josh. He was in his fifties now, wrapped in a blood-stained butcher's apron. His stern face, bald head and paunchy shape gave him a look of grim determination.

For no more than a second, their eyes met in a motionless stare.

Waite hated Josh and Josh knew it. He could feel the hatred cut into him. A sense of terror made him shudder. But the fright didn't stop him from stepping forward, his hands rising almost automatically, holding his driftwood up before eyes that burned with animosity. Henry Waite met the mute's peace offering with an offering of his own. He raised his right hand, pointing it straight at Josh's head, the long silver blade of a kitchen knife extending beyond his fingers. "Get away from my store, you dirty little mute," he hissed, "and don't ever let me catch you bothering my customers again."

Josh backed up, lowering the driftwood to his side, and turned back toward the street. Behind him Henry Waite slammed his door, but Josh hardly noticed. His interest was now in two schoolchildren coming up Main Street.

Two men watched Josh come running down the street, their wooden chairs propped against the front of The Queen, next to the saloon entrance. One of them chuckled to himself as Josh dropped to his knees in front of the children.

"What's that fool Calvert up to now?" he asked his half-dozing companion. "Who cares," the other answered.

The Conlon kids, Johnnie and Sarah, were stunned when Josh ran up and knelt in the dirt in front of them. They were amazed because they'd never been so close to the mute. There was a rumor that years ago a farmer beat Josh for following his kids home from school, so none of the children ever went near him.

And yet here he was kneeling in front of them, his face a little lower than theirs, looking up at them with a gentle and kind expression.

Johnnie was eight, Sarah ten. They lived with their mother in the back rooms of the Sentinel building. Their grandparents, who had started the paper in Shiloh, were both buried in the church cemetery. Neither of the children remembered much of their father. He had died just after Sarah's third birthday. But he was in their thoughts often.

And now, as Sarah examined Josh's kind face, so close to her own, closer, in fact, than she'd been to a grown man in years, she wondered if her father had ever looked at her like that . . . like a beggar, she thought, but a beggar who wanted to give, not receive.

"I'm Sarah Conlon," she said sweetly, "and this is my brother, Johnnie."

"How do you do," young Johnnie said, laying his canvas schoolbag in the street and offering his right hand for a shake. Holding her school books against her chest with both arms in a posture of ease, her yellow hair hanging out beneath the blue-checked bonnet that matched the fabric of her dress, Sarah watched intently as Josh's right hand passed a stick to his left and rose in a slow surprise to clasp with Johnnie's. Sarah's careful gaze didn't miss the shock in Josh's expression. His mouth gaped slightly as he looked from the joined hands to Johnnie's face and back again.

Josh smiled broadly when Johnnie withdrew his hand to pick up his bookbag. "You can't talk, can you?" Sarah asked, wondering what it was like to be mute. As Josh shook his head sideways, a shade of sadness swept into his expression. For the first time, Sarah was aware of the dirt on his clothes and his face. She was about to tell him that he needed a bath when his eyes opened widely and a smile erupted and he began to shake his head up and down, leaning a little closer to both of them to emphasize the change in his answer.

"You mean you really can talk?" Sarah asked, obviously interested enough to hear more. Josh rested back on his heels, smiled even wider and slowed the nodding of his head to a confident rhythm of yes, yes, yes.

"Really?" Johnnie squealed, amazed.

Yes, yes, yes, Josh's head nodded.

"Let's hear," said Johnnie, he and Sarah stepping closer and bending down a bit.

Slowly, Josh's hands rose until he held the driftwood in the center of the triangle formed by their faces. The kids fixed their eyes on it, and Josh pecked at it with his forehead, his eyes darting back and forth between theirs, searching for a hint of understanding, hoping they would see what he so clearly saw.

The three of them huddled in the open street, only two men watching, their silent communion unbroken as the children squinted at each other and the driftwood, wondering what this wordless mystery meant.

"Children," the widow Conlon's voice broke up their game. Suddenly they were gone, sprinting toward their mother, who received them in the doorway of the Sentinel, anxious to hear of the day's adventures.

Josh dropped the stick from the air, not knowing what to do. Twice now his mission had failed. People didn't understand his message. They couldn't hear what he was saying because they didn't trust him, didn't believe anything good could come from a mute. Distrust. Defeat. No! Josh stood up. He would figure out a way to tell them . . . a way no one could fail to understand.

"What's amatter, Calvert; your playmates run away?" A burst of laughter sent this question echoing down the street.

Josh didn't have to face his adversaries to know who they were. The crowd that hung around The Queen never let pass an opportunity to make trouble. His parents had called them "men without purpose." They bunched together, his father had said, only because none of them could face life alone. Josh started to walk away, toward the train station, remembering the long but laconic prayers his father said for the wayward men of Shiloh.

"Where ya goin', Josh; we're just kiddin' ya," one of them shouted.

Josh turned back but kept moving. The two men were standing under the portico, one leaning against the wall,

the other near the edge of the street, his legs in the sunlight, his head and shoulders in the shade. "C'mon back
here, Josh; I wanna see what ya got in your hand." The
request stopped Josh instantly. A flutter of hope filled his
heart. Could it be that they'd understand? Would they be
the first? If he had been chosen, Josh thought, why not
them.

In a minute he stood before them, holding his driftwood
up with both hands, straining with his jaw to make an in-
telligible sound out of air that rasped from his throat.

"Hmmm, that's really somethin', now ain't it," the half-
shaded man remarked to his friend, smiling slightly.

"Josh here's really come on to somethin', ain't he, Bill?"
he asked the other man.

"Sure has," responded Bill, bunching his eyebrows
thoughtfully. Josh searched their faces, nodded his head
yes and pointed down the street, but the men ignored him.

"I'm thinking maybe Dolly and some of the boys oughta
have a look at this. Whadda ya think, Bill?" The men looked
at each other now; Josh couldn't see their faces. "I'm
thinkin' you're right, Tom. We oughta not let somethin'
this important get away."

The first man turned around again and motioned as
they both began to move toward the door of the saloon.
"C'mon, Josh, you gotta show this thing to a couple folks."

Josh looked back to the street, hesitating, not knowing
what to do. A windmill caught his eye, turning slowly
in the breeze. Cautiously, he stepped onto the wooden
boardwalk and shuffled into the dark saloon, past polite
Tom, who held the door open.

The darkness stole Josh's vision. For a few seconds
everything went black. With his sense of sight gone, Josh

felt fear, a deep, menacing fear that caused him to retreat; a strong sensation of fright that moved him two steps backward. His back hit the door. It had been closed behind him. Someone unseen took his elbow, and Tom's voice yelled out, "Hey boys, Josh here's got something to show us."

The hand on his elbow pulled him forward, prodding him to step closer to the source of his fright, further into the darkness.

Josh had never been in The Queen, but he had imagined many times the wicked conspiracies that gripped those who passed through its doors. His father and mother had called it an evil place, setting Josh's young imagination at work, conjuring up images of creatures hiding in its shadows, stirring restlessly in the confines of its unrented back rooms.

And now, as he stumbled forward and his eyes began to adjust to the low light, his mind imposed some of those images on the figures that moved near the back of the saloon. His hands squeezed the driftwood in momentary terror, thinking he had walked into a room of mutants. A small hunchback moved out of the shadows and sent a quiver of fear along Josh's back. But then he recognized that it was only Quinn, a deformed but quick-witted Irishman who worked at the livery stables. Slowly Josh's vision cleared, and he saw that he stood among ordinary men.

The hand on his elbow yanked him again. It was Tom, pulling him toward the bar and a group of men, who were laughing and making quick remarks to one another. The bar was solid wood with a glistening lacquer finish. It came off the wall to Josh's left at elbow height, curved and ran straight back into the darkness. At ankle level a brass rail followed its curve beneath the resting boots of half a dozen men who leaned over their late afternoon drinks.

Behind the bar sat old Carl Elder, his hair whitened with age, in shirt sleeves and a vest, jesting with the men he served. Behind him stood a fascinating array of bottles and glasses that shot a hundred little light beams into Josh's eyes. Above them a large mirror separated two paintings of unclothed women lying on strange red carpets. Their naked bodies startled Josh, and he turned his head quickly to survey the rest of the room.

A dozen round tables surrounded by empty chairs covered the wooden floor of the saloon. A few men sat at the tables, solitary drinkers, maybe strangers like Josh. Toward the back four men looked up from their card game. Hanging overhead, two rows of brass oil lamps shed a diffuse light across the tables and bar. To his left the wall opened into The Queen's restaurant, and to the right, across the saloon, a double-door opening led to the hotel lobby. Josh took all this in as Tom coaxed him to the edge of the bar.

It was Young Thomas, no longer young, almost fifty now, but still the biggest, roughest man in Shiloh, who pushed off the bar and walked around to stand beside Josh.

"What ya got there, boy?" he asked, the other men laughing at his question as they gathered around.

Josh almost whimpered to himself, intimidated by the sinister tone in Thomas's voice. He knew now that Tom had deceived him, that these were mean men with violent hearts. But when Josh thought he would cower and crawl away, he felt courage rising inside. Boldly, so boldly he surprised even himself, Josh swung out from the bar and planted himself, feet spread, face to face with a half-circle of suddenly leery men. With Tom behind him, he thrust his short, dark message up before them. Smiling now, he shook it in their faces, one hand holding each end of it.

"What's that? A piece of driftwood?" one of them asked.

"Yeah, a stinkin' piece of driftwood," Thomas blurted and they all laughed.

"What's it mean, Josh?" the man at the end of the circle asked. Josh sensed sincerity in his voice and moved toward him, running his finger back and forth along the top of the wood as if he were answering.

"It means this town's goin' downstream," someone else said, drawing a few laughs. Josh shook his head, no, still looking at the man at the end of the circle.

A heavy hand grabbed Josh's shoulder and spun him around. Josh dropped his arms, but held his stick.

"You better come clean with us, Josh," Young Thomas stated, draping his hand again on Josh's shoulder. "What's it mean?"

"I'll tell you what it means...." This came from Carl Elder, leaning on the inside of the bar just a few feet from Josh. Elder looked Josh fully in the face, curled his mouth into a cruel grimace, and said, "Josh here's callin' all of us driftwood, ... that's what he's doin'."

Pain shot down Josh's arm as Young Thomas squeezed into the base of his neck, big fingers trying to hurt.

"Think you can get away with that, you no good mute," Thomas yelled. Josh heard others say mean things like that as he bent under the pain. Suddenly his arms began to rise and Josh saw a big hand wrapped around his driftwood. His pain disappeared. Thomas yanked at the wood, but Josh wouldn't let it go. His feet left the ground, swung into the men who kicked at his legs, but still he held on like a fish being pulled out of water. Then Thomas palmed Josh's face and thrust hard, pulling the stick away as Josh fell backward into someone's arms. Suddenly he was propelled back up, and he leaped for the wood high in Thomas's hand. The men laughed hard now as Thomas held the stick over Josh's head, out of reach and made him jump for it like a dog. After a couple of leaps, one of the men kicked Josh in the back in midair. He crashed into a couple of chairs and ended up under a table.

Elder yelled, "You pay for any damage, Calvert." Young Thomas whistled to the yelps of his cohorts, "C'mon, boy; cum git it."

Josh charged at Thomas, who passed the stick to another man. Josh followed, but the stick was already in flight, heading for the card table in the back of the room. Josh turned to run after it when Young Thomas slammed a forearm into his back. The blow sent him crashing, almost senseless, into the tables and chairs. He pulled himself up in time to see a card player fling the shaft of wood back toward Thomas's group. But it hit a ceiling lamp in flight, shattered glass and ricocheted to the floor not far from the opening of the hotel lobby.

"What's goin' on here?" Dolly Elder screamed as she entered the saloon from the hotel. The white frill on the hem of her wide, pink dress swayed as she bent down and picked up the driftwood.

"What the hell you boys up to?" she blurted loudly, everybody now looking her way. The barmen loved her boisterous manners. She was the only woman left in Shiloh who drank with them and wore low-cut necklines. There was a time when her tightly-corseted body fit her suggestive wardrobe like hot silver in a mold, but that time had long since passed.

Dolly knew it but refused to change her style. And now as she sashayed across the saloon, thinning blonde hair turbaned over her head like a younger woman's, her aging body immodestly exposed, the boys encouraged her foolish illusion by acting as if Sarah Bernhardt herself had just walked on stage.

Brazenly flirtatious, egged on by Dolly's bawdy jokes and seductive gestures, the boys warmed to her sensual presence. The queen had entered her court and her subjects were aroused. "Well, Miss Dolly," one of the men called out, using her self-selected title, "Josh here just plain interrupted a quiet afternoon... even broke one of your lamps."

A bunch of them started to laugh, but Carl Elder cut it short. "That's right, honey, this boy's nothin' but a troublemaker."

Josh began to get to his feet and Miss Dolly rounded the tables to meet him.

He reached for the driftwood, but she pulled it behind her back. Josh stood before her, trembling slightly. Her left hand came up and gently stroked the side of his face, her fingers now laced in his curled hair. The boys snorted, stifling their laughter, watching the game intently. "Josh, you're no troublemaker, are you?" Dolly asked, an unusual, motherly quality in her voice.

Josh shook his head no, no, not at all.

"Don't you lie, boy," Young Thomas yelled. But Dolly turned and her stare suppressed his objection. Her strange odor dazed Josh like an unknown incense, and the intimacy of her flesh, displayed so close to his eyes, brought wonder and confusion to his mind.

"I didn't think you meant it. You're too nice a man," her hand now combing over the top of his head.

Her tone was reassuring, so believable, and Josh wanted to believe, but there was something false in her face. Josh could see that her skin was covered with a flesh-colored powder that ended unevenly at her hairline. He could see that her lips and eyes were painted with a paste. There was nothing like this in his memory. His mother's skin was real, but this wasn't. This was a lie.

Then his eyes caught hers, and she knew that he knew she was lying. Fingernails dug into his scalp, and she yanked his hair to the left. He saw it coming, the driftwood, whirling wide in her right hand, but he couldn't defend himself, not against a woman. The stick struck hard on his cheekbone and he fell again as she released him to the floor. Applause and laughter burst forth. "Now get him the hell out of here," he heard her yell, her frilly white hemline brushing over his prostrate hulk as she swept to the bar.

Young Thomas hoisted her up on the dark-lacquered throne as Josh and his driftwood were thrown into the street. The door slammed behind him, cutting off the noise of their celebration.

# CHAPTER

# 7

JOSH REACHED HIS FARMHOUSE just as night fell over the prairie. In the silent little cabin he rested his beaten, but unbroken body on the hard wooden bed. Laying on his back, he watched a circle of candlelight leap up and down the walls and across the beamed ceiling as a draft threatened its flickering flame. Sleep would come, he told himself and in the morning he would find a different way to tell the people of the secrets concealed in his driftwood. He had no choice but to try to make them see. This was the purpose he was chosen for, and he promised himself he'd fulfill it. Comfort came with his commitment and he realized that the peace he had discovered on the Crescent's shore was still with him. And then he slept.

He woke in the middle of the night, hours before dawn, his mind still searching for a way to make his message known. He rose and went to the table his father had made.

It sat by the back wall like an altar in some small, forgotten chamber of worship.

Josh sat in front of the candle and took up the driftwood again. He studied it in the light and saw its meaning so clearly. The lines on its surface and the suggestion of its shape were unmistakable.

His imagination wandered back to the Crescent, and he wondered how long ago its rapids and sluices had first battered its bark away. He thought of the mighty forests so far upriver and sought in its smooth textures a clue of its origins, but found none. He conceived fantasies of the forces that whittled its natural form into its present finish. These thoughts thrilled him because the content of this simple stick was so profound. And what thrilled him most of all was the memory of the moment his gaze first traveled over the bright crystals of sand and fell upon its dense shape. This thought, above all others, filled his heart with gratitude and thanks because he knew its resting place beside the Crescent was no accident. Somehow it had been placed there for him, and only him, to retrieve.

Josh lowered his head to the table and wept, the memories of his struggles and despair draining away with his tears. He prayed for a long time, searching for an answer, looking for a way to explain what the people had to know.

Sincere though he was, concentration fled, and he found himself strangely dwelling on thoughts of his father's death.

He lost so much when his father had died, when he found him frozen miles from the cabin by a sudden and unexpected blizzard, but no sense of loss accompanied his memory tonight. Swiftly his mind moved to his mother's demise, her countenance so sweet that morning she refused to wake at his prompting. Before this moment, thoughts of their deaths disturbed him, savagely plunged him into despair. Strange was the feeling that held him now, so detached and unstrained, though the memories came upon him in vivid detail. Had he triumphed over loneliness? Conquered the turmoil of loss? Had he at last untied those emotions knotted up by the confusing threads of death?

Uncertain, and yet untroubled, his mind alert and not the least bit sleepy, Josh went outside to breathe the cool air. It was black over the prairie, the moon only half its full circle, but Josh could see the woodline across the over-grown pasture, the empty pigpen and the dark outline of the barn. He heard the slow spin of the windmill, rickety in its old age, pumping a supply of water too little for any family to live on. But that didn't matter: his parents were gone.

He walked to the windmill and drank a handful of fresh water. For a minute he thought about repairing the pump, making it suck harder, "but why should I," he pondered, "they're dead and I don't need it...." Josh repeated that to himself and the truth of the thought began to dawn in his mind. He didn't need it. That was it.... His parents once needed this farm, but they were gone.... The farm was of no use because he would be gone soon too.

Josh clapped his hands in the silence of the night. He knew that the farm would serve one final purpose. He saw it clearly now; a vision unfolded in his mind. He would use the farm to show the people of Shiloh the secrets that had been shared with him. His message would be as clear as the spoken word. No one in the town could possibly overlook it, or mistake it, and he would fulfill his mission.

The purpose of his life would be complete.

Moving now with excitement, with the wisdom of an answer that sounded right, he raced to the barn and pulled out the wagon that his parents had left him. He no longer had a horse, but that didn't matter either. He'd pull it himself.

With a lantern lighting his way, he ripped thin strips of wood from the side of the barn and the floor of the cabin, pried shingles from the roof and cut the table into pieces. He uprooted plants and pulled the wire mesh away from the chicken coop. He tore the straw out of his mattress and broke the narrow spindles out of the back of his mother's old rocking chair. He took all of his books, towels, utensils, cups, plates and tools and piled them all on the wagon. Then he stuffed his personal effects into an old carpetbag his parents never used, and threw it under the wagon seat, the last possession he'd take along.

He wished somehow that his parents were with him. He knew they'd understand, even be honored that their son received such a high calling.

He listened carefully and the music of the night brought forth words his father once uttered. "Somewhere, Josh," his father told him, "your voice is riding on the wind, speaking in whispers to people who can hear its gentle sound."

If only he were beside me now, Josh thought, he'd surely hear my voice.

This inspiration accomplished, he spent a quiet moment saying good-by to the only home he ever knew, paying tribute to the experiences and memories this earth, this life, had allowed him to share. And then, before the sun arose, Josh strapped himself into a horse's harness and bent his body to the task that waited in Shiloh.

# CHAPTER

# 8

NOT LONG AFTER THE SUN spread a fresh day over the prairie, the door of the general store opened, and Henry Waite stepped out into the light. He took a deep breath of the crisp morning air, stretched his arms to the sky and quickly surveyed the scenery. Nothing stirred in the early dawn, and Henry liked it that way. He liked being the first one up and out in Shiloh. It made him feel good to know that he got a look at the day before anybody else. As he turned from right to left he anticipated what he would see. Everything appeared as it should be.

To his right, across a patch of open ground, the hardwoods were unmoving. In front of him the church sat motionless. To his left the long street was supposed to be empty, but it wasn't. Henry didn't like what he saw, didn't like anyone disturbing his morning view, let alone a dumb mute. Henry squinted, trying to figure out what Josh was doing, had an impulse to go inside and get his shotgun, but let it pass.

At the far end of Main Street, Josh had parked his wagon, parked it right in front of the old train station, right in the middle of the street. Henry could see the wagon was loaded with junk, but he couldn't make out what Josh was doing in the dirt.

Josh was kneeling, doing something with his hands. The sight ruined Henry's morning, but he wasn't going to waste time trying to stop it. "That stupid fool," he muttered to himself, slamming the door as he ducked inside.

The schoolchildren saw him next, a handful of them, a few from in town and a couple from the farms. Johnnie and Sarah Conlon came out of their home at the Sentinel and spotted Josh right away. Normally they would have cut between the livery stable and the sheriff's office to get to school, but on this morning they passed by their short-cut and walked up to Josh.

He greeted them with a smile, getting to his feet as they approached. "What're you doin'? Buildin' something?" little Johnnie asked, seeing that Josh had laid two long boards parallel in the dirt, separated by about a foot.

Josh nodded his head, yes, yes, yes in reply.

"What's it gonna be?" Sarah asked, her eyes wide with wonder.

Josh spread his arms and began to sweep them back and forth, taking in everything.

"What do you suppose he means?" Sarah asked Johnnie.

"I don't know," Johnnie shrugged, his book satchel rising slightly with his shoulders.

Josh gestured and pointed at the sun. As they watched his hand, he lifted it slowly until it was directly above his head, pointing at the sky.

Two other farm children stood by them now, watching quietly. Josh pointed down at the boards and then up again in the same position.

"What?" Sarah asked. Josh repeated himself, pointing first at the sun.

"You mean the sun?"

Josh's head nodded again positively, and he pointed overhead.

"When the sun gets there, . . ." Johnnie almost squealed, enjoying the pantomime.

Josh bent toward him, smiling brightly, nodding yes, yes, yes, and pointing again.

Suddenly Sarah understood. "We'll see what it is when the sun gets there," she half screamed, jumping slightly to point where Josh had pointed.

They all stared at Josh expecting a quick affirmation. He motioned yes, but just for an instant, then slowly shook out one little no, not quite.

Pointing again, he started overhead and traced the path of the sun down to the mountains in the west.

"We'll know what it is when the sun goes down," Sarah jumped and Johnnie too, who shouted her discovery right back at her.

"We'll know what it is when the sun goes down," he mimicked.

The other children weren't so boisterous. Never taking their eyes off Josh, they backed away a few steps while Sarah and Johnnie celebrated with a few more leaps. Then they all ran quickly around the livery stables, remembering school. Little Johnnie stopped and looked back just before he ran out of sight around the stable's back corner. "Bye,

Josh," he yelled, and then he was gone.

Josh stared at the spot where Johnnie had stood for a
moment, marveling at the beauty and energy of children,
wondering why they changed so much when they grew
up. The old windmill next to the tracks drew his eyes up
toward the grain elevator. He noticed the faint outline of
the word *Shiloh*, almost as gray as the aged wood building,
but speckled with faded chips of white paint that refused
to yield to the slow war waged by the weather. His conscience stirred with the urgency of his message. From the
wagon he pulled a few long pieces of barn siding and an
old saw.

Within an hour Josh had cut a couple dozen short pieces
of siding. As the sun rose and shortened the shadows over
Shiloh, the street came alive with curious people, respond-
ing to the repetitive echo of Josh's hammer which sent its
sharp report along Main Street. Some people opened their
doors and leaned out just far enough to identify the source
of the noise, then disappeared inside. While it was still
early, a few others, not many, ventured to the edge of a
little circle Josh had fenced off. He greeted them all with
a polite smile but was too caught up in his work to spend
time gesturing to them.

With the wire from the chicken coop, Josh had made a
twenty-foot semicircle around the wagon and his work
area. On one side of the circle he had piled up a long mound
of dirt about a foot high. On the other side he dug a narrow
trench. They ran parallel for about ten feet, maybe fifteen
feet apart, with the two boards laying flat in the middle.

Little Quinn, the hunchback Irishman, leaned on a pitchfork in the huge doorway of the livery stables, watching
Josh work. After a time he walked to the edge of the mute's

chickenwire circle, planted his pitchfork firmly in the dirt, and said, "They're not going to like this one little bit, Mr. Calvert. I would suggest that you take whatever it is you're doing out of the street. Otherwise, my wordless friend, you will draw upon yourself an angry mob."

Josh didn't stop to acknowledge Quinn's warning. He looked up for a moment but quickly returned to his work, and the little Irishman soon uprooted his pitchfork and walked away. Josh considered the situation for less than a minute and concluded his mission could not be postponed by fear. But he did appreciate the concern, especially the phrase, "my wordless friend." Josh knew it was an empty expression, but it sounded good nevertheless.

At noon a few wagons went by, but Josh never even looked up to see who held the reins. He stayed busy, diligently hammering together those short strips of barn siding, creating a bunch of odd-shaped rectangles of different lengths and widths.

Early in the afternoon when school got out, all the children came running around the edge of the livery stable, heading directly for Josh. Almost a dozen burst around the corner with festive curiosity, giggling and squealing in a loose procession, but when Josh stopped hammering and looked up in their direction they stopped in their tracks and fell silent.

Josh felt badly about their reaction, but he understood: they thought he was crazy. He smiled and turned back to his hammering.

Sarah and Johnnie took the lead now, the others following until they all spread out around Josh's knee-high fence.

"Hi, Josh," Sarah said.

"Hi, Josh," Johnnie repeated.

A few more hi's and one hello bounced off Josh's back, but he just continued to hammer away, squatting over his target, shielding its shape from clear view. Next to him lay a stack of small boxes, intended for some unknown purpose.

"It's gonna be a ship."

"No, it's a tool chest, isn't it, Mr. Calvert?"

"That ain't no tool chest."

"Probably a watering trough."

"I know what it is. . . ."

"What?"

"A coffin."

The hammering suddenly stopped. Josh stood up, his back to the children, holding something up against his stomach. He paused for a minute and then turned to show them the fruit of his labors.

A gasp of amazement, almost in unison, came from the children, who looked in silent admiration at Josh's handiwork.

Sarah said, "Josh, it's beautiful."

Then they watched Josh walk between his two boards and set on the end of one a small church, a handsome miniature, an accurate replica of the one that sat empty at the end of the street in Shiloh, complete with its own little steeple and cross.

# CHAPTER

# 9

THAT SAME AFTERNOON, Jan Conlon, the widow, was in the back of her house, in the kitchen, baking bread when she heard the knock on the Sentinel's front door. Wiping her powdery white hands on her apron, she passed from her home, through the vacant editorial office, by a room full of wooden type, past the printing press to let in Betty Waite.

Betty came in hurriedly saying, "Have you seen what Josh Calvert's doing in the street?" Her timbre sounded troubled.

"No, I haven't," Jan answered.

"Well, take a look," Betty said, pulling the door open and standing aside to make it easy for Jan.

Before she saw Josh, Jan noticed Young Thomas and a group of his cohorts, including Betty's husband, Henry, talking on the walkway outside the bar across the street.

Jan followed the direction of their discussion and spotted Josh in front of the train station, kneeling in the dirt next to his wagon, busy at something.

"What's he doing down there?" she asked Betty as she stepped back into the printing shop, leading the way toward her kitchen.

"Nobody knows, Jan, but Henry thinks he's just plumb crazy and wants to...." Betty hesitated and Jan picked it up. "Wants to what?"

"Wants to do something about it.... I wish I knew what he had in mind," Betty said, somewhat exasperated.

The two of them settled around Jan's kitchen table. Jan put a pot of tea on the hard iron surface of the stove and Betty draped her shawl over the back of her chair.

Jan knew that Betty was a decent, moral woman. They had tried together, a decade before, to talk the pastor into staying, offering to contribute extra from their savings to keep him on. It was no use, however. The pastor said the town was dying, and the church was one of its last victims. He left town without saying so, but Betty and Jan both suspected he had decided to give up the ministry.

Since then, there'd been little activity in the church. A few weddings, and a few more funerals, one of which Jan remembered all too clearly. Her husband fell to pneumonia not long after Johnnie was born. He was a journalist when they met and married in Colorado. They had moved back to Shiloh to gain experience publishing the paper Jan's parents had left her. But there wasn't much worth reporting in Shiloh, and after his death she devoted her energies to the children. The paper never appeared again.

With a sigh she said, "Henry's a good man. He won't do Josh any harm." Her tone was purposely reassuring.

Betty admired Jan, envied her education and youthful good looks, appreciated her occasional counsel and encouragement. "I know it, Jan," Betty agreed, "but those other men sway him...."

"Now that's just fear talkin'," Jan said sweetly.

"I think there's more to it than fear," Betty added.

"Why do you say that, Betty?" The tea water boiled and she got up to get it.

"Your father wouldn't have let them carry on like this," Betty said, hinting that she knew more than she was saying.

"For God's sake, my father's been dead for twenty years, and you know as well as I that he had no real influence around here." Jan poured dark tea into two cups, set the pot on the stove's shelf and brought the tea to the table.

"But your father spoke out. He had character, like you."

"What's there to speak out against now?" Jan thought out loud. "Dying men hanging around a dying town, threatening to harass a harmless mute?"

"I know you don't mean that, you can't be that...."

"That what?" Jan asked boldly. Answering herself she said, "that cynical, that pessimistic, that...."

"That uncaring," Betty blurted, as loud as Jan, whose voice had risen to Betty's surprise. "Jan, this isn't like you. You're not like the rest of...."

"How do you know what I'm like, Betty? My God, we never talk; nobody ever talks around here." Jan stood up, turned, and sat down, feeling relieved.

Betty's head hung low, facing the table. "Henry talked to Carl Elder and some of the men at The Queen this morning," Betty wrenched it out of herself. "They're talking about killing him."

"Josh?"

"Yes, Josh. Henry said they could drown him in the Crescent, like a rat."

"But why?" Jan asked in disbelief.

Betty's lips pursed and tightened. Ashamedly, she spoke up. "They say he's a curse."

Perplexed, Jan stared at her, a look of disgust on her face. "A curse?" she repeated.

Betty nodded.

Just then they heard the front door open and slam, then immediately open and slam again. The sound of two sets of footsteps raced toward the kitchen.

"Mom, Mom," Johnnie and Sarah cried, nearly out of breath, "it's a town, Mom."

"It's a town," they yelled in unison, breaking into the kitchen.

"Calm down, kids," Jan suggested, raising her hands, palms out to indicate quiet. "Don't you say hello?"

"Hello, Mrs. Waite. Hello, Mrs. Waite," they said.

"Mom, it's a town," Sarah pleaded, so excited she could hardly hold still.

"What's a town?" Jan inquired, trying to look puzzled and interested.

"Josh Calvert is building a town," Johnnie cried, trying to squeeze between his sister and Mrs. Waite.

"A beautiful little town, just like Shiloh," Sarah added.

Jan looked at Betty sadly. Neither knew what to say.

# CHAPTER

## 10

IN THE BAR A STRANGE, virulent silence hung over the sullen
patrons. They had talked long enough. Now they waited.
Bitter words had been exchanged, and the passions of
blood were aroused. All agreed that something must be
done about the mute, but there was disagreement on the
exact action required. Some argued that his death was too
severe a punishment. Others claimed it was a fitting reward for the travesty he created, "turning Main Street into
a sandbox," "playing children's games in the heart of the
city," "disrupting normal life."

"He'd have been locked up long ago if the sheriff were
around."

"No man has the right to turn a town into a laughing-
stock."

"He's been a menace all his life."

"We've got to get rid of him. He's just gonna hang around

here haunting us until we put an end to it."

"He's probably a devil, anyway; probably talks to them all night out there on that abandoned farm."

"That's another thing, the way he let it run down."

"And what about the way he leers at the kids."

"There's a lot more wrong with him than we think."

"It ain't just his voice that's queer."

"Nothing wrong with a man that ain't got a voice."

"But he's different; prowls all over at night."

"He's nothin' but a damn thief."

"Worse'n that, he's evil."

"You can see that in his eyes."

All morning they talked. Vigilantes feeding each other the food of hatred. Dolly stirred them into a fervor with her talk of bewitching spells driving people crazy and curses inhabiting people. Her father told her how to spot them when she was young. Her father had come from New England and learned what to look for from some older uncle or aunt. "There are signs," he had told her, "always signs."

Dolly called up from the past all the signs they'd been given: the train wreck, the drought. Then she brought it all home, up to date, tied the curse together when she pointed her fiery wand of suspicion at "that boy without a voice."

"Hey, Henry, lookie here," called Tom from just inside the door. "Your wife and the widow are headin' for the show. Now ain't that somethin'."

"Let me see," growled Henry, moving quickly from his place next to Dolly at the bar to Tom's vantage point by the door.

"Sure enough, that's her," said Young Thomas, looking through the dirty plate-glass window.

Across the street Betty, Jan and the two kids stepped off

the boardwalk and headed toward Josh. They were already past The Queen, too far for Henry to call them back. He watched them join the small circle of adults and children watching the mute.

Hissing his displeasure, Henry spun and paced back to his drink. Every eye followed him, every ear listened for his answer when Dolly asked, "What're ya gonna do, Henry?"

Jan was startled by Josh's artistic ability. Primitive and slightly rough in composition, the church and the general store he had finished imitated their life-size models with striking fidelity. The church steeple with its perfectly matched belfry and the curved marquee on Josh's imitation of the Waite's store reminded Jan of a priceless miniature Christmas village, all bright with a blanket of white cotton snow, that she had seen once in her childhood when her father had taken her to his home in Philadelphia. They had visited a wonderful department store called Wanamaker's, where dozens of little children looked with fascination at the tiny Christmas village. She thought that with a little paint to match colors, Josh could indeed create a truly artistic reflection of the town.

Betty interrupted her thoughts, "Don't you think that little store looks just like ours?"

"Exactly," Jan answered.

Josh stood up and turned and the kids squealed with delight. Jan felt her heart flutter when she saw what he held—a mirrorlike image of her home. Josh ignored everybody now, intent on finishing his work, but when he knelt to put the Sentinel building in place, a sensation swept over the side of his face. Amid the commotion and exclamations of recognition, he knew that someone was looking at him in an unusual way, like his mother looked at him. He felt the eyes upon him, the eyes of someone with a heart that could hear. He turned his face up and to the side, and there he met her gaze.

Jan's body shuddered when she saw her home in miniature. The effect was inexplicable, as if she had just looked into a mirror and discovered something different about herself, but couldn't determine exactly what it was.

The children were yapping, Betty was shaking her arm in excitement, and the other adults were openly amused, but Jan was oblivious to the whole scene. Something inside had awakened and she was struggling to sort through a myriad of cascading impressions to figure out why, but she couldn't grasp the reins of her emotions. They ran wildly along an unfamiliar road. And then as quickly as they broke loose they settled into a calm, an unimaginable, almost imperceptible peace.

She watched those knowing hands guide what seemed like her life into its proper place on Main Street. She watched his face oversee with unspoken confidence the lowering of the Sentinel to its final resting place, right next to the church and its cemetery. And suddenly she was aware of him, of this unusual man-child who had never spoken a word to her or anybody else, who had lived a life of solitude and pain, she was sure, who had incurred the wrath of Shiloh's men for simply being himself, who had come now bearing such a remarkable and unfathomable gift. She looked at his clothing, so pitifully dirty, and then his eyes and hers met in a channel so complete and intimate she instantly knew, immediately possessed the wisdom that he wasn't what they thought; he wasn't crazy.

Josh bowed his head and turned back to his work, and

she noticed in his movement something that she had almost overlooked in his eyes. His body was worn thin, undernourished, and he looked tired. She wondered what kept him going; if he had been without sleep; how much more he could accomplish.

The stacatto of his hammer flooded her ears, and she was aware again of the sounds of the crowd. Next to her, Betty was ecstatic, "It's so beautiful; but why is he doing it?" she wondered out loud.

"Josh," Jan called across the small circle that separated them. "Josh," her voice traveled over the miniature rooftops and vacant lots of the model city. "Josh," she raised her voice slightly this third time.

People had asked Josh questions all afternoon, but he pretended not to hear, continuing at his work. But Jan's voice carried in it a quality of sincerity that told him to stop hammering. He knew as the words reached his ears, seemingly separate from the noise of the children who darted, cheering, back and forth around the circle, that they came from that woman who had searched his eyes, asking without speaking for some hint of the truth.

Slowly he stood and turned to face her, still holding onto his hammer. Again their eyes met, and it was as if something unknown was transferred across that passage of vision. It wasn't like the earthly love of a man and woman. It had no sensual purpose. And it wasn't secretive, not something to be hidden. It was more like a compassionate understanding that their lives were meant to meet at this moment for a purpose neither could grasp.

Jan broke her thoughts with a question that brought quiet over the crowd. The children stopped in their tracks and squeezed between the adults to watch Josh respond.

They knew he would answer because this was the first time he had stopped working to listen to anyone.

"What does this mean, Josh?" Jan asked. "Why are you building this beautiful little city?"

Without expression, other than a look of physical weakness, Josh lifted his arm and pointed at the horizon to the east. Tracing an arch through the sky, his hands caught up with the sun. It was about 3:30. He let it fall again to his side.

Immediately a murmur arose from the crowd, everybody trying to figure out what he said. Josh's eyes jumped from face to face until he found Sarah, tucked between her mother and Betty Waite. Her little blonde head turned slightly, her brow furrowed, eyes squinched, and then she cried out, delighted to draw so much attention to herself, "He means we'll know tomorrow, when the sun comes up."

The murmuring broke momentarily. Josh nodded his head, yes, just once, smiled slightly and turned back to kneel in the splintered wood and curled shavings of his street-level workbench.

Almost immediately the talk rose again and the children dashed to surround Sarah, the ephemeral heroine who correctly interpreted Josh's peculiar sign. The mood in the air around the mute craftsman was festive. In the presence of the crowd and their pulsating interest, Josh found fresh inspiration. His flesh ached with weariness, but his will compelled him to continue the task. Drinking in the din of the crowd's conversation, listening especially for the voice of that woman, he sensed that his painstaking effort, his precisely detailed work, would draw even more curious spectators tomorrow. And once he finished, once he completed the vision of the small city that unfolded the night before at the farm, he was sure they'd understand the full meaning of his message. His hammer fell with a new devotion, driving a row of small nails through a single shingle that would form the roof of a dwarf-sized Queen.

The party ended abruptly. Without warning a wave of stillness swept over the crowd and splashed against Josh's back. It rolled away like a breaker retreating back to the sea, but an uneasy feeling remained. When Josh turned, he found out why.

The crowd parted like the waters under the bow of a ship, and Josh faced a surly contingent of angry vigilantes, stomping toward him from The Queen.

Led by Young Thomas and Carl Elder, with Henry Waite slightly behind, a dozen men belligerently advanced on Josh's hamlet. His chickenwire fence proved a poor opponent to Thomas's boot, which bent it to the ground in one step. Carl and Young Thomas crossed over the flattened fence, but Henry and a few others stopped outside its circle.

Betty examined Henry's face for a hint of shame, but found none. She stood by quietly, like the rest of the crowd, knowing her objections would fall on deaf ears. Some of the people were already moving away, toward the safety of their homes and wagons. Bravely, Josh took two quick steps forward to meet the assault, to protect his work from destruction. He stopped an arm's length from Elder and Thomas, his feet rooted between his church and general store.

Hatred poured from the faces of his aggressors, who took up positions just in front of Josh. "Calvert," Elder yelled, as if he needed to shout to capture everyone's attention, "you've done nothing but cause trouble around here lately. We've let you get away with a lot of it, but this has gone too far." Elder's judgment drew echoes from his henchmen. Jan was outraged, but fearful, and Betty grabbed her arm to keep her from joining the fight. The children huddled behind the few remaining adults, frightened by Elder's bombast and the threatening presence of Thomas.

"You think you can just come in here and disrupt our city like this, . . ." Elder thundered. "You've got a lesson to learn, boy, and you're gonna learn it now!"

With that, Carl pointed at the general store and Young Thomas kicked it so hard that it splintered into a dozen pieces. The crowd let out a horrified gasp, and Jan screamed "Stop!" But it was too late. While Young Thomas lifted Josh off his feet, another man responded to Elder's snapping fingers by stomping the church into the dirt.

By this time Jan had broken free of Betty, shoved Elder out of her path and was beating on Thomas's back with both hands.

Young Thomas reacted instinctively, throwing Josh with an angry thrust and swinging to swat his unseen opponent. The back of his hand caught Jan on the neck, knocking her into the mound of dirt that represented the mountains to the west.

The crowd stirred, and in its midst Betty saw the shame spread over Henry's face. Even vigilantes knew better than to hit a woman. Elder called his men off, quickly retreating from this inexcusable blunder, their intentions cut short by this uncalculated interruption.

"C'mon, he's had enough," Elder yelled, leading his crew back to The Queen.

Everybody obeyed Elder's command, but one man, who

followed a gentlemanly instinct to help Jan to her feet. This man turned and crossed the fallen fence into the circle where Josh and Jan had been knocked down.

Josh stirred and found himself sprawled across his street-level workbench, laying in a pile of wood shavings and tools. He lifted his head and caught sight of one of the men from the bar entering his circle. Most of the crowd had dispersed, and Josh's stomach wrenched with fear of another assault. Before the man had taken two steps, Josh found himself sitting up, posed defensively with something in his hand. When the man moved quickly to Jan and began to help her up, Josh's fear vanished. Getting to his feet, he remembered the man's face. He was the one who spoke with sincerity in the bar, a good man who intended no harm.

Relieved that the tempest had passed, Josh's eyes were drawn to his hand. A feeling of repulsion suddenly swept over him when he saw the sharp wood chisel, knowing that its purpose could only be violent. His face tightened in reaction to the thought of how he might have used it, and he threw the chisel into the dirt, dropping to his knees beside it.

Covering his face with his hands, he began to weep, searching inside for the poison that had prompted him to take up a weapon, praying that it would never return, knowing that his life must remain separate, not given to the devices of other men. "O God," he pleaded in the silent sanctuary of his mind, "don't let me fail like this again."

A gentle hand rested on his head, and he opened his eyes to look through a veil of tears. He saw a dress with a pattern of tiny pale white horses printed on a light blue cloth. His eyes jumped from horse to horse, across intrusions of dirt from his little mountain range, until he reached the face of the woman who had tried to rescue him. Her children and her friend were now at her side, and a few others gathered around them. The man from the bar was gone, but another man helped Josh to his feet. Most of the crowd had dispersed, and so it was only a small group that stood by while Josh wiped the tears from his face.

Standing right next to him now, with a hand held against the swollen side of her neck, Jan wanted to help Josh recover. She sensed how great his pain must be—united as they were by the swift, harsh ordeal—and wanted to minister to his needs. His face could not hide his weariness, and she wanted to get him home before he collapsed.

Jan spoke openly, unembarrassed by the presence of others or the boldness of her suggestion. "Josh, I want you to come home with me now and rest up. You can take a bath and sleep if you want. We'll come back and clean this up later," she said.

Josh's answer came immediately. He set his chin in an expression of firm determination and shook his head no. Before Jan could protest, he bent over and lifted a hammer out of his pile of wood scraps. Moving slowly but with purpose, their eyes following, Josh went to the fence and lifted it from the dirt. Hammering a small post back into place, he had it standing again in a minute.

Jan and the others, sensing that Josh could not be stopped and not wanting to stand in his way, skirted the fence where it ended by the steps of the train station and left the circle. For a few minutes they watched Josh collect the splintered effects of his miniature village, and then they turned toward their homes, each leaving with a burden of pity and shame.

Just before dark, Jan carried a bowl of soup and a loaf of bread to Josh, who received them with a grateful smile, set them on his wagon, and turned back to his work without even a taste. Jan wanted to scream at him, to tell him to slow down, but instead she found herself near tears when she saw, almost hidden behind a wagon wheel, another perfect little replica of Shiloh's church. While Josh continued to carve on something she couldn't see, Jan left him again and went home.

Late that night, while Johnnie and Sarah were asleep in the next room, she lay awake wondering why she was so drawn to the mute, so fascinated by his unexplainable behavior, so enchanted by his artistic vision, so astonished at his devotion, his pursuit of a dream that only he could understand. She couldn't escape the notion that there was some vital truth, some urgent message at the heart of his obsession.

It must have been after midnight when she rose from her bed, trying to break the spell of her imagination, and went to the front door. Opening it carefully, she stepped into the black night, her thin bedclothes giving little protection against the chill. She shivered as she looked with eerie compassion at the glow of light at the end of Main Street. Moving in and out of a circle illuminated by a lantern mounted on his wagon, Josh carried out his ritual of creation, oblivious to the needs of his body or the eyes watching him now.

No longer aware of the chill, no longer conscious of anything but the enigma she beheld, Jan wished she knew how to help him with his strange mission.

As he disappeared and appeared again across the threshold of light, Jan wondered how many times he had tried to talk to them, how many times he had come before them, only to be turned away, ignored because he did not speak their language. How long had he been among them, she wondered, and how long would he remain?

Quietly she waited, watching each movement, expecting nothing, but drawing pleasure from this secret interlude. After a time, she couldn't tell how long, Jan turned away and the scene slowly faded from her memory. When she reached her bed, she found the arms of sleep ready to draw her in.

# CHAPTER

## 11

THE SUN CLIMBED OVER the horizon and threw the long shadow of the giant windmill across Josh's village. As it rose in the early hours of morning, it drew the rounded edge of the shadow closer and closer to the chickenwire fence. Josh was the only one moving on the street until Henry Waite stepped out for his early morning stretch. But no sooner had the sunlight splashed over the miniature rooftops than the city of Shiloh started humming with life. By 9:00 A.M. there were more horse-drawn buggies in the street than the town had brought together in several decades.

People milled about, crisscrossing Main Street, going in and out of The Queen's restaurant and general store, causing a long-absent and welcome commotion. A small group of farmers gathered in Henry's store, their wives filled the printing room of the Sentinel. Others crowded into the restaurant while their children ran up and down Main Street, creating the illusion that a celebration was underway, as if Shiloh had just produced a record harvest and the farmers were here to load up the grain elevator.

Carl and his wife exchanged greetings with the families who sat in their restaurant. They could hardly keep up with the orders, but they tried, Dolly turning eggs and flipping pancakes on the griddle while Carl went from table to table, pouring coffee from a porcelain jug.

The city hummed with the animation of new life, and all those who took part in it were amazed. Almost overnight, Shiloh had been revitalized, restored to the kind of enthusiasm that marked its daily life in the late 1860s.

And everywhere the discussions were the same. The talk that rose and fell in the restaurant, general store and Sentinel all concerned the same thing. Every conversation held to the same track, a track that led to Josh Calvert and his re-creation of Shiloh.

People asked each other why he did it. They pondered the meaning of his village and offered one another half-baked definitions, unfounded speculations. It did not take long for them to realize that no one really had any idea of what Josh was up to. All of his life he had been a mystery to most of them. Yet nothing he had done was as mysterious as his present behavior.

Word of Josh's undertaking had spread over the surrounding farms in a matter of hours. School-age couriers had carried the news home to their parents and neighbors, and it wasn't long after sunup that a train of buggies was on its way to town.

By now most of them had taken a good look at Josh's handiwork. The small city was complete, intricately carved in just enough detail so that every building was easy to recognize, almost perfect in its proportion to others. The general store and church gave no hint of the storm they had weathered. In lifelike detail, a small corral set off the livery stable at the end of the street. And The Queen, almost a foot and a half high, imposed itself over the other buildings in realistic fashion. Most people felt that the railroad station was Josh's most faithful reproduction. It sat at the foot of Main Street, a quiet testament to the mute's creative powers, a flawless image of the wood frame building that rose from the dirt just a dozen feet away.

The people had come and gone in droves all morning. They all asked questions but Josh never stopped to answer, and they somehow found the respect to fall silent, to watch in awe as he carried out his mission.

The village appeared complete in every way, but Josh continued to work. The mountains to the west and the gorge of the Crescent to the east were the only elements obviously out of scale. Both were miles too close to the tiny hamlet, but their meaning was certainly clear.

For almost an hour, Josh had been sawing small dowels from the round spindles he had ripped from the back of his mother's rocking chair. Finally his saw was stilled. Josh stood up from his work area and drew a deep breath, sucking in oxygen to hold off exhaustion. At his feet lay a hundred small sections of spindle, short, round dowels that would finish the task.

Moving to his wagon, Josh reached deep into the pile of wood that remained and yanked free a large copper kettle. Bending now, he took up his hammer one last time. Holding the kettle in his left hand, he began to slam the hammer flat up against its bottom. The effect was clamorous. The people around his fence covered their ears as the clanging carried an alarm up Main Street.

In a matter of seconds, the street was flooded with people, all coming toward Josh, the farmers in their overalls and black jackets, their wives in the cheap and simple patterns of frontier fashion.

Jan and Betty were among the first to arrive, but soon the fence was surrounded with men, women and children, some peering over and between those who got there first. There were easily a hundred people crowded around that little circle straining to see Josh's village. Children squeezed between adults where they could, the schoolmarm having called the day off due to the unusual events in town. Young Thomas and two others barged into the crowd and pushed their way to the front for a choice view. Their hostility had not cooled, but their leaders, Carl and Dolly, were too caught up in the morning's receipts to stoke the fires of hatred. In fact, the Elders may have been the only people in town who weren't present. They stayed behind, cleaning up the restaurant for the next round of business.

His kettle and hammer useless now, Josh was on his knees by the small mountain range. Against his chest he clutched dozens of small dowels with his left hand, taking them one by one with his right, and laying them parallel at equal intervals in a line heading for town.

The murmur of dozens of hushed conversations rose instantly.

"He's laying the crossties of the railroad track."

"He's building the rail."

"He's laying track."

A few called out questions, but Josh just kept working.

Patiently, the crowd watched him lay his dowels past the tiny railway station and down into the gorge where the trestle had collapsed. "What'sa matter, boy," Young Thomas shouted, "you forget to build a bridge?" A few bursts of laughter stopped short because most of the crowd ignored the remark.

Josh moved back to his wagon now, pausing for a minute with his head down and his eyes squeezed shut, an expression of fear or maybe doubt slightly visible on his face. And then his hands were rooting around under the wagon seat, in a compartment just large enough for his carpetbag and tools. Again the crowd began to talk, asking what he would add next, the town being complete.

The murmuring came to a sudden halt, the crowd fixed momentarily in awe by Josh's strange gesture. His eyes darting furiously now from face to face, he held above his head, both arms upstretched, the driftwood he had found by the Crescent.

Holding it in its high place, he walked around the inside of the circle, giving everyone a closer look at the final piece of his puzzle.

As he moved in front of Thomas, the din of voices rose again and continued as Josh completed the ritual of his walk. As he passed Jan, their eyes met again, and he read pity in her expression. She did not understand. None of them understood. But his moment of revelation had finally come and now he would show them his message of hope.

On his knees again by the mountains, he lowered his driftwood slowly into place on top of his imitation railroad tracks. And as the people shouted their exclamations, "It's a train! He thinks it's a train!" Josh crawled and moved it along the tracks to Shiloh, stopping when he reached the train station, crawling back to the mountains and doing it over again. Part of the crowd spread out, laughing boisterously at the mute's foolishness, but others stayed, mesmerized by haunting memories and the seriousness with which the mute moved the train. The children took their cue from the adults, jumping around yelling about "the dumb mute's train." One of the bar crowd mimicked a conductor yelling, "All aboard. All aboard."

"This isn't a game he's playing," Jan told Betty, "there's something more...."

Betty interrupted, "Jan, look at him. Can't you tell he's completely crazy?"

"No," Jan said sternly, half whispering like the others standing by in quiet conversation. "This is not the work of an insane mind. There's too much thought and purpose here... and he...." Her voice trailed off, but then she spoke up and many heard her. "Josh," she called. He looked up, recognizing her voice. "What does this mean, what are you trying to tell us?"

His work-wearied face dropped toward the driftwood, and he sat motionless for a moment, two dozen people watching him now. "What is it, Josh?" Jan's voice stirred him. He stood up and held the driftwood out to those still watching, and then he pointed, slowly raising his right hand toward the mountains to the west and shaking the driftwood at them with the other. Watching him motion in the noon sunlight, his face pleading for them to listen, Jan finally understood.

"Are you saying that a train's coming to Shiloh?"

He looked at her and pressed his eyes closed as a smile found its way across his mouth. His head nodded, yes, yes, yes, a train is coming. This said, Josh collapsed.

# CHAPTER

## 12

TWO MINUTES AFTER HE PASSED OUT, while two farmers helped Jan carry Josh to her home, news of the mute's claim swept up and down Main Street as quickly as a telegraph could carry it. A good many farmers took their families home, but a small number stayed, gathering in The Queen's restaurant to talk over the day. Carl's crowd held forth in the adjoining bar, and, as the afternoon went on, opinions shuffled back and forth between the two rooms.

When word of the mute's declaration first reached the bar, brought by an eyewitness, a farmer who had seen Josh collapse, the crowd burst into laughter. Dolly expressed their delight with the mute's foolishness like this: "There hasn't been a train over those tracks in thirty years, but who knows? Maybe Calvert is personal friends with the railroad's president."

The crowd roared its approval, some raising their whiskey glasses to toast Dolly's wit.

"They sure got a lot in common," came forth a voice in the crowd, extending the laugh long enough for someone else to add, "Yeah, they both play with choo-choos." That one doubled over a couple of patrons, while others chimed in a chorus of "choo-choos" and "woo-woos."

The reaction of the men in the restaurant failed to reach such revelry. The fact is the farmers were prone to ponder such things, accustomed as they were to reading the signs of nature and occasionally sensing an omen in the change of the seasons.

For them, Josh's prophecy might have some other significance. It was, they agreed, unlikely that a train was coming. But reason suggested there might be a deeper meaning in all of this. Logic told them that a crazy man would not have had the discipline to do what Josh had done.

As their ideas began to crystallize, a fifty-year-old farmer named Mueller emerged as an informal spokesman.

Mueller and his father were two of the men who built the grain elevator and windmill and helped put Shiloh on the map. It saddened him every time he looked at the ghost of the word Shiloh that they had painted on the side of the grain elevator.

Like the others in his position, providing for their families with bare hands, hauling their crops to market twice a year in open wagons across the harsh prairie, taking whatever they could get for their arduous, unrelenting labors— like the others, Mueller did not find much in life that was humorous, and he certainly did not like the idea of taking lightly, no matter how unlikely it sounded, the possibility that a train might be on its way to Shiloh. Like the others, he didn't believe it deep down inside, but he thought the notion worth further consideration.

When he and six of his friends, dressed in similar fashion in black jackets and dark, wide-brimmed hats, got up from their tables and walked through the opening that led to the bar, their presence had an immediate effect. The uproar of laughter died instantly.

Josh became aware of two quickly pulsating sounds. They were close, very close, but he couldn't draw them into clarity. They faded and then came back again as his mind climbed the stairway that rose from sleep into consciousness. One of the sounds paused for a second, and Josh heard a voice whisper, "I think he's waking up." The other sound stopped long enough for a "sssshhhh," and then they were both pulsating again.

Josh realized he was listening to people breathing. He opened his eyes, and there they were, two little oval faces less than a foot away from his, staring at him with a sense of wonder and awe.

"He's awake; he's awake, Mom; Josh is awake," he and Josh.

"He's awake; he's awake mom; Josh is awake," he and Sarah chorused together as they raced from the room.

Josh watched them hurriedly disappear through the doorway into a hall. Sitting up on a small, quilted bed, he took in the unfamiliar surroundings. A single oil lamp, covered by a milk-white glass, hung in the center of the ceiling. It brightened the clean little room which had just enough space for a chest of drawers, a washstand, shaving mirror and towel rack. Josh saw a razor and lather brush sitting next to the basin on the washstand, felt his chin and remembered how long it had been since he'd cleaned himself up. A fresh white washcloth and towel hung next to the washstand, put there for his use, he was sure.

His eyes roved behind the half-open door, where he noticed, to his surprise, a pair of gray pants with black suspenders attached and a fine white linen shirt, all dangling from a hanger that gave the impression it had been hung there for him. The clean clothes embarrassed Josh, making him want to shed the dirt-laden shirt and pants that clung to his body like moss. He noticed that his boots and coat were missing and got up to track them down. He scanned the room again, this time catching sight of several cracks in the paint on the ceiling and a few rips in the wallpaper, which repeated a faded picture of an old brown steam engine.

Suddenly the widow Conlon was standing in the doorway, with another white towel draped over her shoulder, the sleeves of her dress rolled up in working fashion. "I'm glad to see you're up," she said. "The way you passed out, I wasn't sure if you'd ever come to."

Josh just stared at her, unmoving and impassive. "Are you all right?" she asked, realizing he looked dazed.

Josh nodded his head slowly, yes.

"Let me see," she spoke softly, coming forward, her hand rising until her palm pressed lightly against his stubbly cheek. "You feel fine," she said, putting the back of her hand against his forehead. "No fever."

Josh watched her go through these motions in silent disbelief. His eyes followed her face, studied her mouth as each word formed and sprung from her lips. Amazement filled his heart. To think that this woman had opened her home to him, had defended and rescued him. No one had treated him with such kindness, such concern since his mother died. As she turned toward the door, revealing Johnnie and Sarah behind her, Josh felt as though he were going to pass out again and had to sit down on the bed.

"Are you all right?" Jan asked again, suddenly kneeling in front of him, taking his hand in hers, her children coming to stand behind her, one at each shoulder.

His mouth opened as if he could speak and his little audience listened with rapt anticipation. But no words came forth, and he could not tell them of the wondrous feelings he experienced. He could not tell them that he had never been so close to another family, that he had never had a woman touch his cheek or children wait by his bedside. He had never been a welcome guest in another home or felt such love poured upon him. If this were all life held for him, he wanted to tell them, it would be enough. But he couldn't. Instead he tried to put as much thanks as he could into his expression and looked each of them in the eyes, conveying the gratitude that flooded his heart.

His head nodded yes, yes, I'm all right. Relief broke their anxious little circle of faces.

"You can change into these," Jan said, rising and closing the door enough to give Josh a better view of the clothes. "They belonged to my husband, and I've saved them for just this moment," she said kiddingly, lifting the spirit in the room. Sarah and Johnnie smiled at Josh too. Josh smiled back.

"Come and help me fill the tub," Jan said, whisking out of the room, her voice trailing away, "before the water cools."

Josh followed the children into the warmth of the kitchen. Jan was lifting a heavy pot from the stove. "Josh," she said, "you bring the other pot and your bath will be ready." The children staying close to him, Josh lifted the heavy black iron pot and turned to follow Jan down the hall. He could already hear her pouring her pot into a tub that sounded half full.

When he turned, a window surprised him with his own reflection, and he saw for the first time that night had fallen on Shiloh. His mind raced back, and he wondered how many people heard his message. He worried that the town still might not know that a train was coming. Johnnie tugged at his arm, and he moved down the hall into their little tub room. Together he and Jan poured the last pot of water into a white iron-clawed tub, which steamed with an inviting heat.

"Let's leave Mr. Calvert alone now, children," Jan said, pulling the door shut as she lifted the heavy pots out of Josh's way.

Josh undressed and settled into the soothing comfort of the hot water. With a perfumey soap in his hand, he sunk beneath the surface and remembered the fierce under-world of the Crescent. There were black and blue bruises and the cut in his back to remind him of its power. He washed thoroughly and stood up dripping wet, thankful that the river had given him back his life and a message of hope for others.

The towel around him now, Josh stepped out of the soapy tub onto a patch of carpet that felt soft against his feet. He pulled the plug and began to dry vigorously, rubbing his hair with the towel. He felt strong again, manly in a way he wasn't used to, and he noticed the incidentals of the widow's private life. A matching brush, comb, and hand mirror, with a pearllike backing laid amid a collection

of exquisite little bottles, boxes and tubes on a low table
next to another washstand. Traces of a fine, white powder
rested everywhere. Josh sat on a short stool at the vanity
and a mixture of lovely fragrances rose up to meet him. The
tub gurgled as a light tapping on the door interrupted his
contemplation. It was Johnnie with the clothes his father
once wore.

Josh stood in front of the mirror and pulled the black
suspenders over his shoulders, letting them rest on the
white linen shirt. He lifted the widow's brush to his hair
and parted it high to the left. Still damp, his thick black
mop lay flat along the pale line that parted at his scalp.
Lowering the brush, he studied his appearance and could
not find anything in his past that reminded him of this
new image. He had never owned a gentleman's shirt, never
even imagined himself in one. Yet here he was, staring at
himself in an expensive set of clothes, wondering why fate
had decided to dress him like this. The fit was so tailored
Josh knew the clothes were meant for him, bequeathed by
a man buried just a few feet away.

Looking at himself, at this new self, Josh began to feel
that he was as good as the other men in town, that he indeed was their equal. The clothes somehow gave Josh a
sense of identity he had never possessed before, as if they
required that he stand up to the responsibilities of his new
image. And what was this image, but that of a husband, a
citizen of the town.

Somewhat exhilarated, leaving his old clothes piled in
a corner behind the tub, Josh stepped out into the hall, facing the kitchen. An aroma of baking bread and stewing
vegetables filled his head, waking pangs of hunger he
had ignored for several days. The sound of a ladle stirring

against the sides of an iron pot stopped, and Jan turned around to greet him from the stove. Sarah and Johnnie looked up from their seats at the table, surprised by the change in Josh.

"My oh my," Jan said, her voice quivering slightly, "y-y-you look like a new man...."

Her eyes told Josh that she was having some difficulty seeing him in her husband's clothes, and he was about to go to her side when she turned back to her cooking and said, "... but you still need a shave. There's hot water in the basin and a razor on the washstand." All of this she spoke to the wall, her back to Josh.

Sarah added, "You better shave quick. Mom'll have dinner ready in a couple minutes."

Josh went to his room to the sound of the ladle stirring in the pot again. Pulling his suspenders back up over his bare shoulders, he removed his shirt and laid it on the bed. Moving to the washstand, he took up the lathering cup and brush, dipped the brush in the basin of water and stirred up a cup full of suds. Brushing it over his short stubble, he looked at himself again in the washstand mirror. This time he saw a different man, a man stripped to his skin. The razor plowed away portions of the soapy white lather and black beard. Slowly, with each delicate stroke of the blade, his face appeared in its fullness. It was not the face of a young man, not the face Josh had hoped for. It was the face of a man who had suffered much. The lines of age were not hidden, nor were the shadows of weariness. This was the man Josh Calvert was destined to be, not the husband of one woman, the father of children or the citizen of substance. Josh knew that clothes were deceiving, that they had nothing to do with his identity. He looked at himself and despite the sorrow that lived beneath the surface, he knew he gazed at a man who lived for a unique purpose, a man called to a special destiny.

For almost a minute after the six farmers entered the bar, an uneasy silence settled over the room. They stood in a small group by the front door, unafraid, though vastly outnumbered. The barmen didn't know what to expect from them, didn't have any idea why they even came into the bar. No sense offering them drinks or trying to be friendly. Everyone knew the farmers never touched the stuff and didn't care much for men who did. Mueller broke the silence, speaking boldly without a hint of tact.

"You laugh at what the mute has done. We don't." He spoke plainly and loud enough so everyone in the bar could hear. He paused before continuing, but no one interrupted. "That village is not the work of a crazy man," Mueller's voice was firm. Now there were whispers, and short exclamations shooting back and forth all around the bar.

Carl Elder's loud remark brought back the silence as the crowd waited for the farmer's response. "You believe a train's comin'?" Elder asked, his tone indicating it was a serious question.

"We believe," Mueller's eyes scanned the room, "that this is an omen."

Immediately there was an outburst of reactions. The room was filled with the confused dialog of a dozen conversations, some asking what an omen was, others guessing at the meaning of the mute's message. Mueller and the other farmers conferred for a moment, and then Mueller raised his hand, calling for silence.

"We have seen signs like this before," he said, "lights in the sky weeks before a dust storm. . . ."

His audience listened, spellbound by the mystery of his explanation, caught up in the authority of his pronouncement.

"It may well be. . ." he paused, "that a train is coming." His comment went off like a blasting cap, dynamiting an avalanche of debates that raged uncontrolled for thirty minutes. Prairie liquor fueled loud arguments as the barmen sought for a way to laugh off these naive dirt workers. But the doubts had been planted and something stirred deep in the mind of this mob, something they could not explain away or laugh off any longer. Dolly Elder sensed it when she called Josh "nothing but a crazy mute" and had the feeling that she was lying.

A mystery had been turned loose, and it could not be settled by mere conversation. Hard facts were needed now. Something would have to be done to prove the mute wrong. The myth would have to be laid to rest. Hatred and hostility laced the talk that night, but no threat could be mounted, no violence perpetrated until Calvert was proved a liar. Dozens of times voices rose and called for a lynching, but those six farmers standing by the door somehow quelled the fervor of those suggestions. Josh had upset everything and the farmers had introduced the disturbing notion that he might be telling the truth. The anger and frustration in the room finally reached a point where it could not be contained any longer. It was then that Mueller provided the necessary release. "We've got to telegraph Colorado," he shouted, "and find out if there's a train coming or not."

At the dinner table, Jan and Josh sat across from each other, with Johnnie and Sarah between them. In the midst of their small circle sat a large pot of stewed vegetables, steam rising from its inviting brown surface, and a loaf of butter-basted ribbon bread, fresh from the oven. They all bowed their heads and Jan offered thanks for their guest and for the food. After saying amen, she filled four bowls with generous helpings and everybody tore away a portion of the home-baked loaf.

They ate quietly for a time, Sarah and Johnnie spooning up their vegetables and watching Josh dip his bread in the soupy broth. But Jan became uncomfortable. She wanted to know more about her mysterious guest, wished that he could talk and ease her frustration. She knew there was something more than insanity in his behavior.

"Where did you ever get the notion that a train is coming, Josh?" Jan asked.

Josh raised his hand and fluttered his fingers back and forth in front of them.

"At the river?" Jan guessed correctly.

Josh nodded a yes and dipped his head to take in another soppy piece of bread.

"Did you meet someone there who told you this?" she inquired.

Josh responded with a definite no.

"Then how do you know, Josh? There hasn't been a train here in thirty years; the tracks are rusted...."

Josh held his hands up together, cupping an invisible stick, and she stopped, catching her rising tone.

He motioned to Johnnie, who responded instantly. "He means the stick. His little train."

"That's where you got the idea," Jan asked again, "from

that piece of driftwood?"

Yes, Josh motioned.

"And that beautiful little city, you built that just to tell us that a train is coming?"

Josh motioned yes once again. She finally asked when this unannounced train would arrive. Josh shrugged his shoulders and shook his head in a way that said he didn't know.

Jan was silent after that, struggling inside over the puzzle she couldn't solve. Their eyes met several times before they finished the meal and each time she came closer to believing he was telling the truth, despite the doubt that logic forced into her mind.

Sarah leaned over and whispered, "I don't believe a train's coming, do you, Momma?"

Jan said, "I don't know, darling," and her heart wrenched with an intuitive fear.

She fled to the comfort of habit and rose to get a book down from the cupboard. Returning to the table, she sat down, pushing her bowl back and laying open a large Bible. "Every night after dinner," she explained to her guest, "we read a few verses from the good book."

Josh looked at Johnnie and Sarah, and they both continued to eat, paying little attention to their mother.

"We're just beginning the twelfth chapter of Ezekiel," she said, and started to read. "The word of the LORD also came unto me, saying, Son of man, thou dwellest in the midst of a rebellious house, which have eyes to see, and see not; they have ears to hear, and hear not: for they are a rebellious house. Therefore, thou son of man, prepare thee baggage for moving, and move by day in their sight; and thou shalt move from thy place to another place in their sight: it may be they will consider, though they are a rebellious house. Then shalt thou bring forth thy baggage by day in their sight, as baggage for removing: and thou shalt go forth at evening in their sight, as they that go forth into captivity."

Jan's reading had slowed verse by verse until she stopped completely. When she raised her head from the Bible, Johnnie and Sarah were both reaching for another piece of bread, but Josh sat facing her, an impassive but peaceful stare on his face. Again their eyes met in that channel that conveyed something more than words could express. An impression came over her, a prompting to which she yielded, a yearning to believe that the words that she read were somehow meant for him, that her silent guest was present for more than food and shelter.

Her children began to argue over the last piece of bread, but Jan was unaware of their complaints and their spat slowly faded into the cloud of stillness that settled over the room. Once more she looked back at the verses. Each word seemed to strengthen the idea, to support the conviction. Despite the arguments of reason she wanted to believe that verse was a message to Josh. The walls of logic melted before the certainty of this new knowledge, and she suddenly had a hunger to know more, but when she looked up, his chair was empty.

Sarah and Johnnie hurriedly followed their mother down the hall. They found Josh standing in the doorway of the Sentinel staring toward his little city. Jan came up behind him and heard the voices of a group of men. Looking over his shoulder, she watched about thirty barmen and farmers circle Josh's fence, mount the steps and disappear into the dark train station. Their incessant mur-

murs continued to disturb the quiet of the night. When they lit the lamps inside the station, Jan could vaguely see some of them gesturing heatedly to one another through the small paned window of the station's waiting room.

Henry Waite called for quiet in the old train station. Thirty men listened as he tapped out the code on the old telegraph key. Elder, Thomas and the farmers stood over him at the dusty telegraph desk, their backs to the ticket counter and window that separated them from the room where most of the men waited. The dit-dit-dat-dat of metal clicking against metal carried through the still air, every man listening with great seriousness to a cryptic language none of them understood.

Is a train running to Shiloh? Answer key 17.
Is a train running to Shiloh? Answer key 17.
Is a train running to Shiloh? Answer key 17.
The wires carried the unexpected telegraph into the all-night offices at Colorado Springs. Within minutes the surprised key operator, who had to ask an older railroad employee where Shiloh was, sent back a message that Henry wrote down and read aloud. The operator in Colorado obviously misunderstood, thinking Shiloh wanted a train, but his response answered their question. He wired these words: Passage impossible... landslide covered tracks... nature of emergency? Answer key 29.

Elder cursed under his breath, "I knew he was lying." Most of the others shared his sentiment and a new wave of frustration swept through the room. As the train station emptied, the men heading home or back to the saloon, Waite telegraphed back, "No problem, thanks."

# CHAPTER

# 13

JAN PUT SARAH AND JOHNNIE in bed and walked with Josh down Main Street. She knew that he wanted to see what the men were doing, and she was curious too. She didn't think they would do anything violent if she were along, not that Josh was intimidated. He showed no sign of fear. She was reassured when they reached his miniature village. The fact that the men hadn't destroyed it gave her even more courage. She and Josh stopped at the fence just as the men started coming out of the station.

The first one out yelled at Josh as he circled the fence with two or three others. "You're a lousy liar, Calvert; there ain't no train comin'."

Jan moved closer to Josh and took hold of his arm. The men passed by, but others emerged, making the same kind of comments, calling Josh a "no-good liar." Jan noticed tears welling up in Josh's eyes, his only reaction. She shouted back, "He's not a liar!"

The farmers made a quiet exit, and the lights inside the station went off. Elder, Waite and Thomas stepped out of the darkened waiting room onto the station porch, pulling the door shut as they did.

"What're you doin' with him?" Young Thomas hissed at Jan. "You're no better than a whore." The accusation shocked Jan and almost took her breath away. She squeezed Josh's arm and hid her face behind his shoulder.

"Thomas here don't mean no harm, Miss Conlon," Elder insisted, "but you really shouldn't be seen with such a fool if you're lookin' to preserve your... ah... reputation."

Jan regained her composure and looked up as the three men came around the fence toward them. "You see, Miss Conlon," Elder continued, "Josh Calvert is nothing but a pitiful little liar."

"Stop it," Jan screamed, to no effect. Suddenly Josh turned in exasperation and pointed directly at Elder's face. The three men stopped, slightly surprised by the mute's action.

"Don't get yourself all worked up now," Elder said, "just 'cause the whole town knows you're crazy."

Elder laughed. So did Thomas. And as they turned up Main Street, Henry Waite uttered viciously, "There ain't no damn train comin'," and cast a piece of crumpled paper at the mute's feet.

Josh picked it up and gave it to Jan. With three voices laughing in the background, she unfolded and read the telegraph message that contradicted his prophecy.

It was dark in the empty street. The sounds of several buggies faded into the night. Faint noises found their way from The Queen to the street, but even Elder's boisterous laugh sounded far away, like the sound of a distant cricket.

Josh and Jan were left alone in the darkness that hung over Main Street. The prairie sky shed just enough moonlight to make the tears on Josh's face glisten.

"Don't cry, Josh," Jan said, trying to conceal the hurt she felt, "what you've done is . . . beautiful. It's beautiful, Josh, even if there's no train coming."

Josh looked quickly into her eyes, fear on his face. His expression grew more intense, and he wept openly, without a sound, shaking his head no, no, no, looking at the ground.

"Josh, please don't, . . ." she tried to comfort him, reaching for his shoulders, but he pulled back. Her husband's old white shirt blurred in the air as Josh jumped the fence. In an instant he was back in front of her shaking his driftwood in her face.

"Josh, stop that," she spoke firmly but impatiently, trying to bring him to his senses, "there's no train coming."

She was adamant, but so was he. Dropping the driftwood, he grabbed her by the shoulders and shook her. He pulled her within a foot of his face and stared into her eyes. He could see that she was frightened, so he released her. She stepped back in response and watched him point down the track, nodding his head yes with renewed determination.

"But Josh, the pass is blocked. . . ."

Reminding him made her feel bad, but she felt she had to do it. Somebody had to straighten him out. Again Josh shook his head no. She wanted to explain it to him, to convince him of his folly, but she couldn't. He stood there in front of her, a man fully persuaded of the validity of his course, pointing toward the mountains, nodding his head yes, yes, yes, the train is coming.

Suddenly she was crying and running away from the man in her husband's clothes. She couldn't agree, and she couldn't stand to disagree any longer. She ran home and tried to hide from her concern for the mute. But the anguish she sought to escape roared into her room like a midnight locomotive, screeching and steaming through a quiet country station.

Unable to sleep or reconcile the cold denial of the telegraph with a mysterious yearning to believe, she walked down the hall to the room where he had slept. She went in and sat on the edge of the small, creaky bed and prayed that her emotions would settle into the peace that passes all understanding. She asked for wisdom in the name of Christ and sensed the presence of God around her. No revelation came to her then, and she went back to her own room, leaving the austere little chamber vacant once again.

# CHAPTER

# 14

THE MORNING SUN BROUGHT a handful of farming families into Shiloh again. Several said they were giving their kids a ride to school, but they had really come to see what the mute would do next. By 9:00 A.M., there were almost a dozen buggies parked along Main Street. The general store and The Queen's restaurant played host to most of the visitors.

At one point or another, everybody made their way down to Josh's miniature hamlet and watched the mute run his driftwood train along the tracks, repeating his message over and over again.

An hour later, with a group of twenty onlookers, Josh ripped up the fence and threw it on the wagon. Within the hour everyone came back in small clusters for a closer look at his handiwork. Some of the men kneeled in the dirt and poked their fingers into the tiny doorways Josh had carved.

In the meantime, Josh was careful to hold his driftwood up to every visitor, to give them each a close look at the source of his inspiration, to beg each one with his eyes to believe he was telling the truth. His efforts were greeted mostly with expressions of pity or chuckling reminders that the pass was closed.

By this time most of the people thought Josh was genuinely off balance. The general theme of conversation that morning insisted that the telegram proved he was wrong, and it was only a matter of time before he'd have to be put away.

Strangely enough, it was Dolly and Carl Elder and Henry Waite who wanted to "let the mute have his fun." Young Thomas didn't have much patience with their softened position, but he held his desire to tar and feather Josh in check.

Jan brought Josh something to eat just before noon and found a heavy, solemn look on his face. She could see he was stirring inside, trying to argue his way through some conflict. He forced a smile onto his face and set aside the food she gave him. They sat together on the steps of the railroad station, watching in silent communion while people came and went up and down Main Street.

Josh watched a farmer unhitch his horse and lead him across the sunlit street into the livery stable. He watched others crisscross the rutted dirt thoroughfare, busying themselves with nothing in particular, enjoying the show he staged for them.

Deep inside he burned with a dull ache. It wasn't a physical pain, it was the hurt of unreturned love. All these farmers in their proper black coats and hats, their wives in long-sleeved, low-hemmed prairie dresses, all of them, he thought, wishing it weren't so, will be left behind. The townspeople too, and the children, oh the children, tears welling in his eyes now, why can't they see it. He looked at Jan and even though he wanted them all to believe, it hurt him most to think that she, too, would be lost. Tears ran down his cheeks.

He saw the confusion in her face and knew that she didn't understand. Once more he reached out and took her by the shoulders to try to shake the truth into her. It was no use. In her eyes, in her expression, he found only pity. He understood now that she thought he was breaking down. She thought his tears were the outpouring of a disordered mind, a mind racked with confusion and fear, and he had no way of telling her the truth. He cried because no one believed there was hope for Shiloh. He cried because the people went about their business as if nothing had happened to their town. They couldn't see, they wouldn't see that he offered them freedom, that he held up before them a message of liberation. He looked again at the street and saw a half-dozen people who wouldn't believe there was a way out.

The sun beat down on his imitation town, and he knew all at once that his mission had ended. His work wasn't in vain, he told himself, for every last one of them understood what he was told to tell them. Despite their mocking doubt, he never wavered in his conviction that a train was coming. He didn't know where it would take him but he was certain he would step on board. When he was gone, they would know he had told them the truth. He had done all that he could. He had made his message clear enough for each of them to deny it.

The fact that he was mute made no difference. Had he

been the most eloquent orator or even a writer of rare power, his message would have had no more impact than his small city had. In Josh's mind it became clear that despite his flaws, life had molded him into the perfect instrument to pass this news on to Shiloh. He understood with an assurance beyond reason that as mysterious as his behavior seemed to those watching, he had walked the narrow path meant for him. Like the mighty waters of the Crescent, he was forced to flow with the lay of the land by laws he could not change. Now that he had etched his message into the history of the prairie, the moment of his departure had come.

He stood up and took a step.

"Josh, where are you going?" Jan's voice told him that somehow she knew they had reached a point of parting.

Looking back at her, but only for an instant, he pointed again to the mountains. He took the three short steps to his wagon and pulled his parent's old carpetbag out from under the wooden seat.

Jan was beside him again, looking into his eyes, searching for a way to get through. "Josh, you can't leave."

He wished he could say, woman, I can't stay. But he made no gesture at all, just looked at her sadly and walked away, heading up Main Street.

Watching him walk up the center of the street, people stopping and coming out of the buildings to stare at him, Jan felt a strange sense of familiarity come over her, as if she had witnessed this scene before. An elusive feeling held itself just beyond the reach of her understanding as she gazed at this most unusual and sensitive man, walking away from her, baggage in hand, dressed in clothes once worn by her husband. She sat again on the steps of the station and rested her face in her hands.

By the time he reached The Queen, Main Street was lined with most of the people in town. A few made wise-cracks—Young Thomas yelled, "Hey, Calvert, the train station's back that-a-way"—but most remained quiet. As he walked further south, the people spilled in behind him, following him as if they intended to say their good-bys when Josh passed the church. The barmen, farmers and their women formed a throng behind him, some of them laughing at Thomas's jokes.

Much to their surprise, when they reached the church and the final group of bystanders on the porch of Waite's General Store, Josh turned around and walked right back into the crowd, which parted before him like the waters of the Red Sea.

When Jan saw the crowd open and Josh emerge, coming back down Main Street toward the station, a phrase sprung into her mind, but disappeared before she could grasp it. The scene she beheld was overwhelming. It moved toward her with an eerie sense of finality, unlike anything she had ever experienced, as if it had some higher purpose and lasting significance.

The street of Shiloh was crowded with a parade of people marching two steps behind a leader they thought insane. Josh's linen white shirt, brightly lit by the afternoon sun, stood out in sharp contrast to a background of black jackets, brown vests and other dull frontier fabrics. The whole crowd was laughing now, mocking the man whose short march had made him look more ridiculous than ever. She could hardly believe how unreal and sad life had become. This small little insignificant town had nothing to do but celebrate the insanity of one of its poorest inhabitants.

And then that phrase sprung into her mind again and this time she grasped it. She let the words roll slowly over her tongue, and as they did, they changed her perception of the scene. She heard herself say it again, "... bring forth thy baggage by day in their sight. ...."

Her thoughts suddenly spilled in on her, full of clarity and revelation, and words like *Ezekiel* and *God* and *Josh* and *truth* filled her mind.

She was up and running now, past the unknowing parade, headed for home.

In her bedroom, packing a suitcase for herself and the children, thoughts about where they would go and how they would live didn't matter enough to hold her attention. She fixed her mind on the train's arrival and hoped she could get the kids before it pulled out of the station. She had no idea of exactly when it was coming, but she sensed the urgency of the hour. A powerful, confirming peace filled her heart and she knew now the mute was a divine messenger and that it was only by God's grace that she was able to believe. Nothing else mattered now. She would openly display her belief.

# CHAPTER

# 15

JOSH PAUSED FOR A MOMENT when he reached his little village. He stopped long enough to let the crowd pour in around the hamlet, forming a semicircle just about where his fence had stood. They all looked at Josh, more than fifty of them, and his eyes raced from face to face, finding only insincerity where he hoped to find faith. Their laughter pounded at his ears as Young Thomas's gang shouted for insult honors.

As Josh walked down his miniature street and mounted the steps of the real train platform, a volley of sarcastic good-bys drew a roar of approval.

"So long, Josh, drop by anytime."

"Give my regards to the conductor."

"Remember to write."

"Hope you meet somebody nice on the train."

One of the men started moving through the crowd yelling "Tickets please," reaching out to take imaginary coupons from laughing customers. Another cupped his hands around his mouth and shouted, "All aboard. Next stop, St. Louis."

Josh reached the top step, walked to his right under the portico, and then turned to look at the crowd from the height of the platform. They had gathered as if to send one of their favorite sons off to war.

His eyes roamed the crowd, and suddenly he was staring into a face that understood. All the sounds of the crowd faded, and in an instant he knew that this farm woman believed him. Her eyes reached up at him in silent compassion, and he smiled slightly in her direction. Unnoticed by the others, she closed her eyes and bowed her head. Josh knew she bore the shame for the way the crowd was treating him.

He searched further but found no other believers. And then one of the men from the bar drew his stare. It was the same man who had helped Jan to her feet when Young Thomas knocked her down. Josh wasn't sure what the man thought, but he sensed a hunger and a fear in his gaze, a desire to know the truth.

The crowd opened and Josh had a clear view of the man and there at his feet lay the driftwood, amid a dozen scattered dowels from the imitation track.

The man looked down, following Josh's stare. When he looked back up, Josh nodded yes and then turned away.

A group of men climbed the steps behind Josh and followed him as he walked along the porch, rounded the end of the station, and walked out onto the long platform where the trains once loaded and unloaded their passengers. The boards of the platform were warped and buckled from years of disregard. Josh dropped his carpetbag and stood in the sunlight, halfway between the back windowed-wall of the station and the edge of the platform where the tracks ran. Several of the men following Josh sat down behind him on the old wooden benches along the station wall. The portico that wrapped around the station cast a shadow over their seats, dividing them from Josh by a line of shade.

Most of the crowd circled the station on the ground and crossed the tracks to watch Josh and those with him from the edge of the prairie. Like actors on a stage, Josh and the other four men on the platform fidgeted around before the curious gaze of their audience. The tracks that separated them were silent. One of the men took to looking at an imaginary pocket watch, shielding his eyes with one hand like an Indian, squinting toward the point where the tracks emerged from the mountain, thirty miles to the west.

"I guess the old one-fifteen is runnin' behind schedule," he shouted to the crowd's delight. "You reckon' it'll get here soon, Josh?" he shouted. "I gotta important meetin' up in St. Louis." The audience roared its approval.

Josh looked nervously up the track and then fixed his gaze on some invisible point out across the prairie, praying quietly that something would happen soon. He had a strange feeling that the joking wouldn't go on much longer. He didn't know where it would lead, but the crowd made him uneasy. The men on the platform were under pressure to perform, and he could sense they were searching for something even funnier.

The crowd's attention shifted momentarily away from the station to a point up Main Street out of Josh's vision. Somebody was coming. The men behind Josh moved over to the edge of the building just as Young Thomas emitted a long two-tone whistle. A few of the barboys tried to out-do one another with spontaneous "wahoos."

Josh knew the object of their admiration would arrive any second. He saw the parasol first, a pretty light-blue thing tipped toward the sun. Dolly and Carl, all eyes on them now, ended their promenade next to the railroad tracks at the end of the station. They faced the crowd and Josh could see no more than the expensive red-silken, white-frilled dress that spilled out from under Dolly's small umbrella. A few farm women whispered to each other, and Josh got the distinct impression that there was disgust in what they said.

"What's goin' on, boys?" Dolly asked the gathering, more or less ignoring the women present.

"Miss Dolly," yelped one of the men on the platform. "Miss Dolly," he said it again, quickly, turning her and her husband, arm in arm, fully in Josh's direction, "me and Calvert here's jist waitin' on the old one-fifteen."

Dolly laughed out loud and the rest of the crowd joined in as the man moved over to Josh and slapped him across the back, saying, "Ain't that right, Josh?" They all laughed again. Even the humorless farmers found something amusing in the impromptu skit. Josh stood firm, staring at the Elders.

"I didn't know Mr. Calvert could afford a train ticket," Dolly declared. "I didn't know he owned anything but the dirt under his fingernails."

Carl Elder and the barmen roared at this, but the farmers found nothing funny about her reference to working the land.

Josh could hardly believe the appearance of the Elders.

Carl was dressed in a vest and gambling coat made out of a thick silvery cloth, offset by a pair of black pants and a dark hat. Dolly wore a dress so tight in the waist and low in the front that her breasts were squeezed upward, almost spilling like pinkish lemons out of a fiery red pitcher. They were dressed extravagantly for midafternoon and Josh couldn't understand it. Even across the twenty feet that separated them, Josh could see the lines of color painted on her face, the dark red lips, the silvery-blue paste under the eyes, the rouge on each cheek and the pale pink powder caked underneath everything. Her blond hair was piled above her head like a turban, all shaded by her diminutive parasol.

Young Thomas and a few others accompanied Dolly and Carl across the tracks to join the rest of the audience, while the men on the platform hovered around Josh, repeating their strange antics, each of them pretending to have pocket watches now, continually asking one another, "What time you got? What time you got?"

Josh tried to remain calm, but his fellow actors kept slapping him on the back, throwing their arms around his shoulders and asking foolish questions like, "Is it true your traveling companion is a wild boar?" "How long have you known the conductor?" "Will you be supping tonight in the dining car, or will you be dining alone in your berth?" For some reason, each question had to be punctuated with another slap on the back, which evoked a small round of mirth from the crowd.

None of this bothered Josh much. What caused him concern was the serious discussion between the Elders and Young Thomas. The three of them kept looking at him while they talked and Josh couldn't escape the notion that

they hated him now more than ever. When Elder waved
Thomas away and the big man drew two of his sidekicks
out of Josh's sight, a tremor of fear swept through his
limbs. He stood silently amid the commotion on the platform, praying that a train would come. He watched Henry
Waite pull his wife Betty through the gathering until he
reached Elder's side. They exchanged muffled comments,
peering at Josh as they did.

The crowd's attention was suddenly diverted again.
Josh couldn't see the source of their shift, but he saw surprise on their faces. All eyes turned toward the livery stable
as Jan came around the corner, suitcase in hand, leading
her children, their classmates and the schoolmarm toward
the train station.

When Miss Hunnicut, the teacher, caught sight of the
crowd, she immediately commanded the children to stop.
They obeyed, gathering around her, but Jan pulled Sarah
and Johnnie with her, along the side of the livery stable.
The crowd began to murmur and point, and this embarrassed Sarah and Johnnie. They didn't understand why
their mother dragged them from the classroom so hurriedly, telling Miss Hunnicut, "a train is coming." The
other kids had laughed and snickered, even after the
teacher said, "Why don't we all watch the train arrive."
Sarah knew Miss Hunnicut was being mean. Nobody in
the little room believed a train was coming. She had told
her class, much to their delight, that Josh Calvert was "not
to be taken seriously."

As her mother yanked her from her small wooden desk
and Johnnie rose to follow, Sarah remembered the words,
"misguided and deceived." These were words the kids
had recently heard, and she wondered if they'd use them

against her mother. Johnnie was crying now, crying, "Mom, let's go home," and it made Sarah angry. Right there, in front of most of the townspeople, on that space of street that ran between the stable and the station, Sarah decided to state her independence. Digging her heels into the dirt, she pulled free of her mother's grip and hissed angrily, "Mother, what are you doing? There's no train coming and. . . ."

"Sarah," Jan cut her off, summoning into her voice the full measure of her authority, "give me your hand and stay by my side. You will see the train," she paused, "soon enough."

She offered her right hand to her daughter, who hesitated. Sarah turned to look at Johnnie, who sobbed in confusion and clutched tightly on her right hand. Then she looked back at her classmates, who were crossing the tracks to join the farmers and townsfolk. She couldn't see Josh, but she knew he was on the platform, waiting for his imaginary train. Finally she lifted her eyes to her mother's face. The late afternoon sun made her squint as she looked up and found love in Jan's expression. Still she hesitated, because there was something else in her mother's face too —a vacant, yet peaceful quality that was new to Sarah. It made her think of those hateful words, and she wanted to yell, "It's not true."

"Sarah," Jan said again and the daughter's hand rose in response, linking their family in a delicate tension. As soon as Sarah surrendered, Jan turned, the suitcase bowing her slightly to the left, and led her children past Josh's miniature creation up the stairs of the station.

When the school kids entered his field of vision and crossed the tracks between him and the old windmill and grain elevator, Josh looked hard for Johnnie and Sarah. Mothers emerged from the mass of faces to draw in their children. But no Jan. It puzzled him that they weren't there, but then he heard Sarah's voice and a moment later the sound of a woman's wooden-heeled shoes beating against the train platform. For some reason the men of the platform faded back onto the benches against the wall.

Josh didn't know whose footsteps were coming. But his hopes rose as they carried closer to the edge of the station. He heard a sob and the sounds of lighter, less determined feet and his heart suddenly leapt as Jan and her children came into view. Tears burst forth at the sight of her and, despite the eyes of the audience, she dropped her suitcase, and they met in an embrace of joy.

There passed between them an unspoken assurance, each knowing their lives were held in unshakable hands. The commitment they shared was rooted in the revelation that had been delivered to the town. They twirled once and clutched one another in a communion no one watching could fathom. When they separated, smiling, she looked full into his face and said, "Josh, I know it's true. . . . I believe all that you've said." Then she placed her suitcase next to his, gathered her children to her side, glanced once at the four men behind her on the benches and turned boldly to face the prairie.

In their union, Josh sought to escape the fear he felt, but it grew instead. Jan's behavior seemed to disgust the crowd. Wild discussion broke out among them. From the platform the mute and the widow listened to the rising tone of their malice. Fragments of conversation reached their ears.

"How dare she involve herself in this. . . ."

"The damn whore. . . ."

"Lost her mind too."

"Did you see the way they hugged?"

Betty Waite pulled away from Henry and crossed the tracks to talk to Jan. Stopping at the edge of the platform, her head even with Jan's knees, a sense of urgency in every word, she pleaded, "Jan, take the kids and go home before something awful happens. . . . You don't know what you're doing."

Josh looked at her and she looked down at Betty.

Her children clung to her dress, burying their faces in its folds. With a hand on each of their heads, she answered Betty, "It's going to be all right, you'll see."

Her serenity brought Betty to tears.

"Betty, it's all right," she repeated, softly, her voice almost buried by the crowd's rising murmur.

Again Betty looked up, summoning another plea from the depths of her heart, but just as she uttered, "Please, Jan," her husband grabbed her arm and pulled her back into the crowd. He tried to comfort her, but she wept, thinking her friend had been deceived, even mesmerized by some wizardry commanded by the mute.

# CHAPTER

# 16

AT THE SOUND OF HEAVY boots falling on the platform Josh and Jan turned toward the corner of the station. As the sound grew louder, the crowd fell silent and Josh's heart beat faster. He glanced back toward the west, then up toward the unmoving windmill, but found no sign of deliverance in either direction. The boots pounded closer, their noise now thundering in Josh's ears, amplified by the hostility of the crowd and the fear in his heart. Sweat formed on his brow, and he placed a hand on Jan's shoulder to comfort her. Closer came the beating sound.

Josh knew it was Young Thomas even before he rounded the corner. But when he came into view with two henchmen behind him and a long leather whip coiled in his hand like a snake, Josh's knees weakened, and he heard Jan gasp.

Thomas and his men stopped, and he lifted the coiled

whip until it pointed directly at Josh. The tension between them erased everything else from Josh's mind. He stared into the eyes of his adversary, and there he found a compassionless rage. "You've made a mockery of this town," Thomas uttered in a slow, heavy way, "and now you're gonna pay for it."

He was vaguely aware that the other men were circling around him, slightly conscious of the frightened whimpers of Jan and her children, oblivious to the cries of provocation from the mob, for all of his attention was concentrated on the face of the man who held the whip.

In this nightmarish scene, the face of Young Thomas became a storehouse of hatred. The lines that spread from the corners of his dark eyes and mouth and crossed his forehead were tracks left by years of a hostile grimace. His thick nose and lips were scarred and flattened by the futile offensives of the hundreds of nameless men he had beaten over the course of his life. His heavy jowls sprung from a neck as solid as the trunk of a hardwood, and the bark of his skin was pocked with the marks of a brutal past. Josh's eyes searched for a passage that would lead to the heart of this hate-filled man, but there was no room for love in the hardness of his countenance, no sign of a conscience behind his awful mask.

Thomas let the leather uncoil and sprawl on the platform at his feet. Jan screamed and leapt toward him, but two men jerked her out of the way, her children clutching after her. Josh tried to move toward her but his arms were suddenly locked in the grips of men stronger than he. He pulled and yanked and pushed with his legs, but like the Crescent, they controlled him and quickly arrested his motion.

Josh stopped fighting and looked again into the face of Young Thomas. Desperately he tried to cast off his fear. He struggled to subdue the hatred that welled up inside him, fought off an urge to hiss and spit at his captor.

The whip rose and curled in the air over Thomas's head. The arm that held it arched forward to lash it back toward its silent target. As the slashing leather snaked through the air, the hatred fled and Josh understood why this must be. In that eternal second before pain shattered his thought, Josh heard a still, quiet voice whisper that "the truth shall set you free."

The whisper faded and Jan's voice flooded his ears with a pleading scream of "Noooooooooo... !"

A burning sting suddenly cut across the center of his scalp and traced a fiery path of pain down his spine where the end of the whip bit into the small of his back. His body wrenched up in a spasm of shock, his eyes bulging at the sky, his mouth stretched wide in a scream that never came. The knots of the whip lashed back toward Thomas, and Josh felt the warm blood in his hair as he collapsed between the men who refused to let him fall.

His vision blurred, he couldn't focus on the sea of faces beyond the tracks, but he sensed their primitive mood. The crowd seemed smaller, and he knew that some had run from the horror. Those who remained offered no mercy. Their clenched fists shook; their voices rose and fell. Before him a light blue blur jiggled in the sunlight and spun like a child's pinwheel and the whip fell again. It caught his head sideways, turned as it was toward the crowd, and crisscrossed his skull with a vicious sting. Again and again the leather snake lacerated his back, and blood soaked the shreds of his white linen shirt and dripped into the gray fabric of his pants.

The widow's screams were muffled by a coarse male hand. She sobbed as Josh finally passed out under the assault of pain. The men would not let her go to him. Instead, they held her between them and accused her of the vilest adulteries. And as they voiced the slanderous imaginations of the town, her children listened, clutched together on the bench where they were forced to sit.

"Get him off the platform," bellowed Young Thomas, dropping his whip and moving to help carry out his own command.

Josh regained consciousness as his bloody body was being pitched back and forth by two mighty men, who shouted in unison, "One."

Josh was lifted forward, his arms stretched wide by the two men who were pulling on his bloodied wrists. His chest was thrust out momentarily, then snapped back by the shoulders as the men reversed their motion.

"Two," they yelled as he pitched backward, his arms almost joined straight out in front of him. Once more they yanked, and his torso leapt like a puppet jerked to attention by its strings. This time his feet left the ground as his chest passed beyond his outstretched arms, but instantly he was whipped back as the men gained momentum in reversing their rhythm.

"Three." They yanked his arms apart and his body pitched up into the open air like an eagle rising in flight, wings spread, hanging for an instant above the watching crowd.

Josh had no control over his fall and he slammed into the dust like a tree falling in the forest.

People crowded around his motionless body, examining the welts and lacerations on his back through the rips in his shirt.

He heard Carl Elder say, "He's not dead. He's hardly even hurt."

"What a pity," a woman added.

Josh lifted his face from the ground and a patch of dirt clung to his bloody cheek. He brought his hand up to wipe the grime from his lips, but smeared it instead. His hand shook in weakness, a burning pain in his back sapping away his bodily strength. He was aware of the crowd standing over him and heard in the din of their conversation, almost imperceptibly, the voice of a woman sobbing in despair. He knew her tears were for him but he was sure no one else did.

Looking up from his prostrate position, he found that he was only a few feet beyond the railroad track. Above the rusted steel rail, standing at the edge of the chest-high platform, Young Thomas and several others peered down at him, disdain in their faces, a formidable barricade to his desire to climb back up on the platform. The whip coiled in Thomas's hand was ready to strike.

Craning his neck, pushing his chest up from the ground, he looked for Jan, but she was not on the platform. Her children were still sitting there, wrapped in fear, but she was nowhere in sight. Then he noticed that the door of the station was open and that the men who were holding her were missing too. He pulled up his legs so that he was kneeling on all fours. Stretching a hand toward the track, the pain in his back like a searing fire, he doubted that he had the strength to rise. Voices taunted him.

"Be careful crossin' those tracks, Calvert, you might get run over."

"You might make the four-o-one if you hurry. . . . But I'm not sure there'll be any seats left."

"Stay where you are, boy," came from Young Thomas, who let his whip uncurl so that it hung down in front of Josh, a swaying reminder of its tortuous intent.

Josh's other hand was on the track now. He gripped the rough steel rail, leaned forward slightly and shook his head, trying to steady his sense of balance. Drawing a leg up, planting his boot in the dirt, he prepared to rise when a tremor arrested his motion.

In his state of weakness and pain, he wasn't sure if he really felt it or had conjured it up, so he held himself perfectly still. There it was again, a distinct vibration, a silent pulse of life raced through the rail under his hands and disappeared down the line. His body stiffened at the surprise and a fear mixed with joy moved through his chest. In reaction, he found himself sucking hard for air as if the breath had been knocked out of him. His mind was suddenly free of the wracking pain and his thoughts raced with clarity. No one else had heard or sensed what he had, no one else knew that from a great distance someone had just sent a message to Josh, timed perfectly for the moment his hands rested on the track.

He stood now, fully assured of the sovereignty of his calling and turned to face the mountains. Shielding his eyes from the slowly setting sun, he provoked the crowd to laughter as he searched the tracks for evidence of an approaching train. The shadows of the mountains already cast darkness over most of the western prairie, but Josh could find no hint of a train to the west.

Dropping his hand from over his eyes, he turned to face Young Thomas. The big man glared at the mute, grimaced hauntingly and flicked his whip to crack out a warning. The crowd backed away as Thomas threatened to lash his victim again. Josh stood his ground, silent but unafraid, knowing that it would all be over soon.

He stepped up on the rail and when he did, Thomas cracked his whip fiercely, yelling, "Stay there!"

But Josh disobeyed, stepping into the middle of the tracks, his beaten, bloodied face and frame a pitiful match for the hulking strength of his enemy. For a second their eyes met and Josh's mouth curled into a slight smile. Pity and love replaced the fear in his expression, and he knew Young Thomas would hurt him no more. Hate had had its moment, and now the man with the whip stepped back, knowing that he couldn't stomach to lift his hand again, thinking that it was wrong to beat someone so insane.

The crowd too sensed that their price had been extracted, and they began to fidget when they realized how far things had gone. Before their eyes a harmless, speechless man had suffered an unwarranted cruelty, and they somehow knew that they were responsible. They huddled together, not knowing what to do next, several women weeping now, wanting to go to the mute, but too ashamed even to offer him help.

And then she appeared. She came out of the station sobbing uncontrollably, clutching the side of the doorway, her dress ripped open from the neck to the waist.

"Mom," her children shrieked, crying and running to her side, the whole crowd watching. Josh mounted the platform as the two men came out of the station. What had they done, he wondered, but the crowd knew, and the men became the release for their guilt.

"You're disgusting," yelled Dolly Elder at the two of

them and turned with her husband to lead the way back up Main Street. Young Thomas swatted at one of the men with an open hand as they left Josh and Jan alone on the platform.

Josh went to her and pulled her away from the doorway, leading her and the children to a bench. He soothed her with loving gestures and caresses and brought her out of hysteria into the peace he had picked up from the vibration in the track.

For a moment she had trouble believing this was real. She could not understand why she had allowed herself to be drawn into this illusion. Here they were, two beaten people, waiting alone at a train station, for what? Her answer came quickly when she saw their baggage sitting side by side and realized that her faith was beyond reason, that the revelation hadn't come purely by logic, but from a source that allowed even this tragedy. She clutched Josh now, and found in their embrace a refuge from the fear that she had done something wrong, made some mistake. She held her children, comforted them and cried when Sarah asked if the train was on its way.

The crowd was almost gone now, except for a few stragglers, curious to see what this unusual couple would do next. The sounds of doors slamming, of boots moving on the boardwalk and wagons rolling on Main Street suggested the day was over.

And as one man watched, Josh helped Jan button up her dress as best they could and then, with the kids following, picked up their baggage and moved to the far end of the platform. Josh peeled off his shirt and Jan did what she could in the receding light to clean his wounds.

# CHAPTER

# 17

STANDING BY HIMSELF in the lengthening prairie shadows, watching them all alone, was the small hunchbacked Irishman named Quinn. He worked at the stable cleaning stalls when he worked at all, but mostly he drank himself into ever deeper debt at the saloon. Considered a quick wit and tolerated mainly for his humorous tongue, he had lingered for an uncluttered look at the couple now silhouetted by the prairie dusk.

Like everyone else he had witnessed their suffering and now, unnoticed, he alone paid silent tribute to the strength they had shown. Quinn admired people of endurance, insane or not, and these two certainly possessed it in abundance.

They stood there, Josh facing west, Jan daubing at his back, the children sitting behind them with the baggage. Quinn nodded farewell as he stepped up onto the outer rail. With a quick hop, his short legs carried him to the second rail, where little Quinn got the surprise of his life. That steel track sent a vibration up his leg, and he looked to the west in stunned disbelief.

A dozen denials rushed into his mind, and he faltered from the rail. Squinting and rubbing his eyes, standing between the tracks, he muttered and stammered but couldn't bring himself to confess what he saw. He whose tongue was usually fluent had to force himself to say, "O my God, it's a train."

On the tracks that had been still for thirty years, tracks that had long been rusted over, Quinn saw a pinpoint of light emerge from the mountains, and he ran up Main Street screaming, "It's a train. It's a train."

His voice carried like an alarm into every corner of the quiet hamlet. The farmer Mueller, with his wife and kids in the buggy, was more than a mile past Waite's General Store when Quinn's shrill voice reached him. He pulled hard on the reins and turned his buggy around near the edge of a hardwood grove and headed back across the flatlands toward Main Street. A look of excitement that he couldn't comprehend came over his wife's face. Then she looked at him, bowed her head and started to cry. Stoically, he refrained from asking her what was wrong, figuring she just wanted to get home. With a lash of the whip he drove the horse to run across the open plains. Mueller could see two other farmers racing their buggies back toward Shiloh, back to the urgent news of Quinn's unceasing cry.

Six buggies converged on Main Street almost at once and ran into a scene of pandemonium. The street was filled with panic. People running toward the train station, grabbing one another, screaming out their desperate questions.

"Who's on the train?"

"Who could it be?"

"How could Josh have known?"

No one had answers. Confused and frustrated beyond measure, Young Thomas suddenly stopped as he ran down Main Street and turned to find Carl Elder.

Coming out of The Queen at a brisk walk, Elder and his wife, still holding her parasol even though the sun had set and the light was soft, stepped down onto the street and made their way around a buggy, where Young Thomas blocked their path. He glared down at the pudgy little man in the fancy silver jacket and spoke harshly. "You told me he was lying, but you were lying," Thomas said.

"I wasn't lying; you read the telegram," Elder's rebuttal was quick. "None of us believed it and you know it."

"C'mon, Carl," Dolly tried to pull him around Thomas, but Thomas stepped to the side and cut them off again. A half dozen people came by, including Henry and Betty Waite who steered around them when they saw Young Thomas shaking his finger in Carl's face. "You lied to me, Carl," Thomas said accusingly, somehow convinced that Elder knew more than he admitted, "and I beat the man for you."

"Ya didn't beat him for me," Carl shot back, angry and unafraid. "Ya beat him 'cause ya wanted to."

Suddenly Thomas swung and caught Carl on the side of the face with the back of his hand. Dolly backed away as her husband spun with the force of the blow, crashing into the side of a buggy, holding himself up on its wheel.

When Carl turned, Thomas was almost at the station.

Wiping blood from the corner of his mouth, Carl scurried with Dolly down Main Street to meet the train. The platform was packed with people crying out to one another for explanations and Carl and Dolly joined a small group waiting on the ground at the edge of the station. Except for the buggies and horses, Main Street was empty now.

Along with a couple dozen others, the Elders leaned out over the tracks for a look at the train coming toward them. All they could see was the intense glow of its light, which beamed brightly over the fifteen miles of flat land that still separated it from the small stop. Against the shadows of the hills, it appeared much brighter than the train lights Carl remembered, but then it had been thirty years since he had seen one. He figured there had been some improvements.

On the platform somebody said the railroad had probably dispatched a train because of the telegram. Within a minute everybody repeated the explanation, adding that the pass probably wasn't closed after all.

"Probably just a mistake in the telegram," offered Henry Waite. "It's easy to misunderstand Morse code."

But though they offered one another reassurance, the growing ball of nearly blinding light hurtling toward them undermined every explanation.

Ten miles now and people wondered why they couldn't see the black outline of the engine or the billows of steam rising from its stack. The glow of light kept coming, growing, obscuring any vision of the train that pushed it forward.

"Must be somethin' new."

"Yeah, it's a brand-new model."

The tracks now vibrated severely. Unused and un-

mended for so long, their bounce was visible. They clat-
tered against the spike plates that held them loosely in
place.

In panic, somebody screamed, "Ask Josh who's on
board." But their cry was lost in the mounting din of a hum
that sounded like the voices of ten thousand people sing-
ing hmmmmm in perfect unison. It carried a feeling of
awesome power but nothing in it suggested the rhythm of
wheels, the throbbing of steam or the meter of steel beating on steel.

When the train was eight miles away, Josh turned
around to face the crowd. Ten feet of empty platform lay
between Josh and the rest of Shiloh's citizens. He saw their
fear and wished for a moment he had more time to share
with them. But there wasn't any time left, and no one had
the courage to approach him after what had happened that
afternoon. Still shirtless, suspenders dangling from his
pant tops, he pointed one last time at the approaching
train and quickly turned to face it, his raw red back a grim
reminder of their unbelief. Jan never turned but fixed her
gaze on the fulfillment of the mute's prophecy.

At five miles, the shape of the train became apparent for
the first time. All eyes were upon it. Some people leapt
from the platform and crossed the tracks for a better view.
The engine had the appearance of an old steam engine,
but every pipe and attachment shone. The whole train was
like a bright light and the light itself, mounted on top of
its cylinder shape, glowed like the sun.

Four miles now and the sound became almost deafening, burying screams of panic, of desperate questions, of
voices trying to explain what was happening to their small
prairie town.

Three miles and the crystal glow of the engine captivated every eye, growing brighter with every turn of the wheel, threatening and yet fascinating as it hurtled toward its gasping audience.

At two miles, the people realized how fast the train was traveling, faster than any train had ever approached their small station. Where was the screech of brakes, the high-pitched squeal of steel skidding over steel?

Almost at once the people understood that this train wasn't braking, wasn't going to stop for Shiloh, would roar through their hamlet like an express that couldn't afford to postpone its mission, that had a timetable of its own, a destination unknown.

One mile left and the radiant apparition raced toward its moment of reckoning with the wild-eyed assembly. The crowd on the platform pushed back furiously, afraid to be too close to the edge, slamming a farmer and his wife against the large paned window of the station, breaking it beneath their weight. As they fell through the shattered glass and wood, no one heard their screams or turned to help them.

Every eye fixed now on the whiteness speeding toward them, its engine visible in bright detail, a glowing spear of slatted steel sweeping along the tracks, the enormous cylinder of the engine hurtling above, the light housing, smokestack, bell and piping before the engineer's housing.

Light leapt from the engine and the two passenger cars like a burst of flame over spilled kerosene. Josh and Jan stood with their backs to the screaming crowd, their bodies sharply silhouetted against the train.

And then it was before them, hurtling through in a dazzling, luminous stream of light, with soft glistening edges on every detail of its image, with a brightness beyond that of the sun, yet harmless to look upon, crystalline and pure and shimmering in its excellence, sending rays of warmth and enchantment to the senses.

There were faces in the windows of the passenger cars, faces that would stand forever in the memories of those who beheld them, faces for the most part unknown, but there among them, as everybody on the platform would later recall, was the face of Josh Calvert, looking out in a peaceful, wishful, glowing gaze of love.

A horn suddenly broke the overwhelming hum of voices, a loud brassy blast that sounded just as the last car passed through the station, and it ushered in the roar of a hard wind that blew down upon Shiloh and sent the old giant windmill spinning for the first time in thirty years.

Every head turned to trace the path of the mysterious white train as it disappeared like a phantom where the tracks curved into a hardwood thicket just a half mile east of town.

The wind kicked up a cloud of dust and for a brief moment, the people shielded their faces from the sand in the air.

And then a single voice screamed with a curdling revelation that turned every head to the west once again. "He's gone."

Where Josh, Jan and the children had stood, the people beheld the strange sight of Josh's carpetbag and the widow's suitcase unattended. The crowd raced toward them, and the man from the bar who had helped the widow was the first to arrive. He knelt in front of the luggage, opened

Josh's bag and then the suitcase and found nothing but clothing and articles packed for a trip. A small circle gathered around the baggage and someone asked where they went. Someone else claimed they must be hiding, but the man from the bar said, "No, they're not hiding. The train took them."

Children were crying now, and the clamor of their voices rose against the mechanical clatter of the old windmill as it slowed again to stillness. Small pockets of people stood on the platform and the prairie, arguing over what had happened. All of them began to talk at once, agonizing and quarreling over the mystery. In no time, they were shouting at one another, ignoring the children, fearful yet belligerent in their opinions.

A shingle fell from the roof of the grain elevator and startled a few people. The wind had ripped it loose, and it landed in the dirt next to a chip of white paint, one of the last specks to fall from the name of the town painted high on the side of that first building.

Suddenly Mueller came running up to the small circle around the baggage, nervous and out of breath. The crowd fell silent. "Have you seen my wife?" he pleaded for a positive answer.

"No, I haven't seen her."

"Have you?"

"No, not me."

Someone finally said, "Last time I saw her she was with you."

Tilting his head back and lifting his hands to the sky, Mueller shouted his wife's name and dropped to his knees, muttering some kind of emotional prayer. His scream surprised the small gathering, and they realized she must have been taken too. A whispered murmur rose from the little circle.

A shout from the end of the platform turned everybody back toward the east. Little Quinn, the courier who had piped the news of the train's arrival, suddenly realized what everyone else had overlooked. "The train must have crashed at the trestle," he yelled, leaping from the platform and running along the tracks toward the Crescent.

"The gorge, of course—it'll crash, . . ." said the man who had opened the baggage, sprinting from his little circle in pursuit of Quinn.

Mueller got to his feet, jumped off the platform and ran after him.

Within minutes, Young Thomas and the rest of the barmen, Carl and Dolly Elder, Henry and Betty Waite, the farmers and their children were walking rapidly along the tracks that led to the gorge.

Just beyond the grain elevator, Dolly found her parasol, mangled and torn by the whirlwind that had sucked it from her hand.

Puzzled and argumentative, unable to comprehend the extraordinary events of the day, the crowd that wandered the tracks wrestled to free themselves from the anguish of guilt and the feeling that they had denied the truth. Belatedly, they were saddened that the mute was not around to answer their questions.

Less than a half mile from the gorge, the farmer, the hunchback and the man from the bar stopped the crowd along the tracks.

Mueller stood with his head down, staring at the ground; the barman gazed away at the darkening horizon; the small Irishman told them what they had discovered in the gorge. "There's nothing there, nothing at all," he said. "The train has disappeared."

In despair the people trudged back to town, and night drew its dark blanket over the prairie, leaving Shiloh almost vacant and silent.

The only sounds on Main Street were the sporadic regrets echoed by the townspeople as they passed Josh's miniature hamlet on their way home, each looking at the driftwood he had offered them, each wishing they had believed the simple message he spoke.

Those who remained would discover others missing in the days ahead. And they would argue about what to do with Josh's miniature hamlet and the driftwood he left behind.

*About the Author*

George Hirthler is a free-lance writer/producer living in Atlanta. He
has also been president of Graphic Truth, a ministry created to spread
the gospel through contemporary media. He is a graduate of Temple
University in Philadelphia.